THE ROYAL BALLET SCHOOL

Diaries

3

Isabelle's Perfect Performance

THE ROYAL BALLET SCHOOL

Diaries

3

Isabelle's Perfect Performance

Written by Alexandra Moss

Grosset & Dunlap

To Amanda Moxey, for all her help and enthusiasm—A.M.

Special thanks to Sue Mongredien

GROSSET & DUNLAP
Published by the Penguin Group
Penguin Group (USA) Inc., 375 Hudson Street, New York, New York 10014, U.S.A.
Penguin Group (Canada), 10 Alcorn Avenue, Toronto, Ontario, Canada M4V 3B2
(a division of Pearson Penguin Canada Inc.)
Penguin Books Ltd, 80 Strand, London WC2R 0RL, England
Penguin Ireland, 25 St Stephen's Green, Dublin 2, Ireland
(a division of Penguin Books Ltd)
Penguin Group (Australia), 250 Camberwell Road, Camberwell, Victoria 3124, Australia
(a division of Pearson Australia Group Pty Ltd)
Penguin Books India Pvt Ltd, 11 Community Centre, Panchsheel Park, New Delhi - 110 017, India
Penguin Group (NZ), Cnr Airborne and Rosedale Roads, Albany, Auckland 1310, New Zealand
(a division of Pearson New Zealand Ltd)
Penguin Books (South Africa) (Pty) Ltd, 24 Sturdee Avenue, Rosebank, Johannesburg 2196, South Africa

Penguin Books Ltd, Registered Offices:
80 Strand, London WC2R 0RL, England

Series created by Working Partners Ltd

Copyright © 2005 by Working Partners Ltd. All rights reserved. Published by Grosset & Dunlap, a
division of Penguin Young Readers Group, 345 Hudson Street, New York, New York 10014. GROSSET
& DUNLAP is a trademark of Penguin Group (USA) Inc. Printed in the U.S.A.

Library of Congress Cataloging-in-Publication Data

Moss, Alexandra.
 Isabelle's perfect performance / written by Alexandra Moss.
    p. cm. — (The Royal Ballet School diaries ; 3)
 Summary: In their second term at the Royal Ballet School, Ellie and her friends prepare for an
important appraisal of their dancing while also trying to get along with Isabelle, an unfriendly new girl.
 ISBN 0-448-43769-4 (pbk.)
 [1. Ballet dancing—Fiction. 2. Interpersonal relations—Fiction. 3. Boarding schools—Fiction. 4.
Schools—Fiction. 5. Royal Ballet. School—Fiction. 6. London (England)—Fiction. 7. England—Fiction.]
I. Title. II. Series.
 PZ7.M8515Is 2005   Keep in Juv. /1/07   or
 [Fic]—dc22
                                      2004029309

10 9 8 7 6 5 4 3 2 1

Chapter
1

Saturday, January 4th

Dear Diary,
    Not long now until my second semester
starts at The Royal Ballet School! I'm so
psyched about seeing all my friends there
again, and getting back to ballet classes,
of course!
    I've had such an amazing Christmas
vacation, what with being one of The Royal
Ballet School students chosen to dance with
The Royal Ballet in the Nutcracker at
The Royal Opera House (it was so
unbelievably awesome, I still get goose bumps
thinking about it) and Mom and Steve
getting married!
    It's taking a little bit of getting used

to, having this whole new person in the family when it's been just Mom and me for so many years, but it's good. Steve is so much fun and I just love it that he so obviously ADORES Mom. He has excellent taste!

I've had tons of fun hanging out here at home in Oxford staying with Phoebe while my parents were on their honeymoon. I got to spend time with Phoebe's new high-school friends, who are really cool.

Christmas Day itself was great, too. Mom and Steve had just gotten back from Spain, and were all lovey-dovey. I pretended to be a bit grossed-out whenever I caught them kissing, but secretly, I thought it was sweet.

And Mom took Bethany and me to see Birmingham Royal Ballet dance Swan Lake yesterday as a treat. It was soooo wonderful. The ballerina who was Princess Odette was amazing—really graceful and beautiful. All the time we were watching, I just so wanted to be her!

Still, right now, I guess I wouldn't trade

places with anybody. I <u>am</u> about to go back
to The Royal Ballet Lower School, after
all. Lucky, lucky me!

I'd better dash. I'm not even dressed
yet, and Mom has called me for breakfast
twice already. This time tomorrow I'll be
having breakfast at The Royal Ballet
School again—yippee!

Ellie Brown waved and waved until her mom's small blue
car had disappeared into the woodland of Richmond Park, out of
sight. Then she turned and gazed up at White Lodge, the beautiful
old building that was home to The Royal Ballet School's Lower
School.

Ellie grinned, feeling a surge of excitement as she looked up
at the beautiful building. Oh, it was good to be back! And she
couldn't wait to catch up with all her ballet friends. She'd said a
quick "hi" to them as she and her mom had carried her luggage
into the dorm, but now her mom had gone, and it was time to
catch up properly!

Ellie hurried over to the huge entrance doors. It was hard not
to *skip* with pleasure as she entered the gorgeous stone building
again, like so many dancers had done before her: Darcey Bussell,
Dame Margot Fonteyn, Dame Antoinette Sibley . . . the list of
former Royal Ballet School students was legendary. And secretly,

Ellie dreamt that in years to come, Royal Ballet School students might speak *her* name with the same reverence.

"Hi, Mrs. Hall!" Ellie called out cheerily, seeing the Year 7 housemother crossing the foyer. "Did you have a nice Christmas?"

Mrs. Hall smiled over at her. "Lovely, thanks, Ellie. How about you?"

"The best," Ellie told her. "But it's even better to be back here!"

"That's what I like to hear," Mrs. Hall said. "I'll come up to the dorm to see everyone later, okay? You can tell me all about it then."

"Okay," Ellie replied as she turned toward the Year 7 dorm. She grinned to herself as she remembered the start of the previous term here, when she'd been a new girl, unable to find her way around the sprawling, labyrinthine school building. Now she knew her way to every studio, classroom, and dorm; she knew everybody in her year—and a lot of the older students, too. She'd even *danced* with some of them on stage, at The Royal Opera House!

Ellie pushed open the dorm doors, knowing that she must have the most idiotic grin plastered over her face. She couldn't help it; it was just so wonderful to be back. "Hi, guys!" she called, rushing into the long, crescent-shaped dormitory that was a bedroom for all the Year 7 girls.

Even on a cloudy January afternoon, the room was light and

airy, thanks to the enormous high windows that lined the outer curving side of the dorm. And there was her bed and her wardrobe and her posters—and best of all, there were . . .

"Ellie!"

"How was your Christmas?"

"Tell us *everything*!"

There were her friends, running over to her: Grace, Sophie, and Bryony. They'd only been at The Royal Ballet School together since the previous September, but there was something about living with friends, dancing with them every day, seeing them at their best and worst, that made Ellie feel as if they'd all known one another for years. As an only child, Ellie had always longed for a sister, and now it felt as if she had a whole bunch of them!

"Hi!" she cried, hugging them in turn. "Happy New Year!"

Everyone was talking over one another, news and gossip spilling out in a rush. Ellie was especially close to Grace, who she'd known from The Royal Ballet School's Junior Associate program before they'd started at The Royal Ballet School. They'd spoken on the phone to each other most days of the vacation, but it still wasn't the same as being together.

Other girls were shouting greetings down to Ellie from the far end of the dorm—Alice, Scarlett, Megan, Holly, and Rebecca. There was so much to catch up on! As Ellie called a happy "hello!" back to them, she noticed something strange. Something different. The halfway space had gone!

During their first term, the beds in the long narrow dorm had been split into two clusters by a much larger gap halfway along, between Lara's and Megan's beds. The girls had taken to using the space for practicing dance steps and doing exercises. On Ellie's side of the dorm were Bryony, Sophie, Grace, herself, and Lara. And on the other side were Megan, Alice, Scarlett, Holly, Kate, and Rebecca. Now the halfway space was taken up by another bed.

"Oh!" Ellie gasped. "Is a new girl starting this term?"

"It looks like it," Sophie replied, looking over at the empty bed, as if she half-expected the new girl to suddenly materialize on top of the blankets. "Seems funny to think we won't be the newest students in the school anymore. Compared to her, we'll be old hands!"

Bryony smiled, her delicate features lighting up. "I love that we're not the newest people," she said, bouncing happily on her bed. "I still had that *wow* feeling when I walked in downstairs, but it was like coming home, too."

"Hm-mmm," Grace agreed, "it's as if we all belong here now. I've stopped expecting to wake up and find that the whole thing has been a dream. This is just what we *do*—live and study at The Royal Ballet School!"

Ellie lay on her bed and stretched one of her legs high in the air. "It's totally cool beyond words," she sighed happily, gripping her foot with one hand, to pull her leg closer to her chest. "I can't wait to start ballet class again." She lowered her leg gracefully, and then flipped over onto her stomach. "Hey, did you guys do much practicing over the holidays? Sophie, were you doing your foot exercises? Be honest, now!"

Before anybody could answer, the dormitory door swung open and in came Mrs. Hall—followed by a girl with a trendy suitcase with matching purse. Everybody stopped talking at once and looked. The new girl had arrived!

She had long, glossy dark hair that swung around her shoulders as she walked, reminding Ellie of a shampoo advertisement. Ellie stared in admiration at the girl's smart black suede coat, fashionable jeans, and glossy black high-heeled boots.

"This way, Isabelle," Mrs. Hall said, leading the new girl farther into the dorm.

Isabelle looked neither to her left nor her right as she followed Mrs. Hall, trailing waves of perfume behind her. Ellie found it impossible to read her expression.

"Your bed is right here," Mrs. Hall said, showing Isabelle the newly installed bed between Lara's and Megan's. Then she looked around the dorm at all the expectant faces. "Everybody, this is Isabelle Armand. Isabelle, this is Sophie, Ellie, Grace, and Bryony."

"Hi, Isabelle," Ellie and her friends chorused. Ellie gave the new girl a welcoming smile. What fun to have a new person starting at The Royal Ballet School!

"And over here," Mrs. Hall continued, "we have Megan, Holly, Scarlett, Alice, and Rebecca. Lara and Kate haven't arrived yet; you'll meet them later." Mrs. Hall smiled reassuringly at Isabelle, and then addressed the room again. "Girls, Isabelle has come to us from Paris. I hope you'll all make her feel very welcome."

As everyone smiled and nodded, Ellie watched the new girl stare rather coolly around the dorm. She didn't seem particularly happy to be there. Maybe she was just shy.

"I'll leave you to unpack then, Isabelle," Mrs. Hall told her. "I'll pop back in a little later to see how you're settling in."

"Hello, Isabelle!" Sophie called over as Mrs. Hall left the dorm. "Welcome to The Royal Ballet School. I love your coat!" she added, in her usual direct way.

Isabelle dipped her head slightly in Sophie's direction, and then bent to heave her large suitcase onto her bed.

"Do you want a hand?" Ellie asked, jumping up to help.

The new girl looked at Ellie with intense dark eyes. "Thank you," she said, stepping aside to make room for Ellie to help. Then she shrugged off her coat and looked around for somewhere to hang it. Ellie could smell the newness of the suede, and wondered if it had been a Christmas present. Her fashionable sweater and pants looked like they came right off the runway.

"Over here," Grace said. She went over to show Isabelle the coat pegs inside their wardrobes.

Isabelle hung up her coat gracefully with a perfectly manicured hand.

Grace hesitated a moment, then held out one of her own nail-bitten hands. "I'm Grace," she added shyly.

Isabelle merely nodded her head in acknowledgement, and

then bent down to unzip her boots.

Grace dropped her hand a little awkwardly, then stepped back, an uncertain smile on her face. "Well, er . . . welcome to The Royal Ballet School," she said. "You'll love it here."

"Really," said Isabelle flatly, raising one perfectly shaped dark eyebrow as if she didn't believe a word of it. Then she pulled off one of her long, high-heeled boots in a single movement.

Ellie stared down at her own scruffy sneakers, then back at Isabelle's immaculate boots. Were *they* new, as well? *Everything* about Isabelle was pristine and glamorous. Still, Ellie thought to herself, once school began, Isabelle would be wearing the regulation school clothes, just like everybody else. High-heeled boots were definitely not part of the uniform!

Bryony tried next. "So, you're French, are you, Isabelle?" she asked conversationally. "My parents took me to Paris last summer. It is such a beautiful city!"

Isabelle tossed her thick dark hair over one shoulder. "Yes," she said simply. "It is."

"And you've been studying ballet in Paris until now?" Bryony went on. Ellie could tell that her friend was beginning to feel a little awkward. Isabelle wasn't exactly doing much to help the conversation along!

Isabelle stuck her nose in the air. "Yes," she said again, "where they know how to dance the ballet *properly*!"

"Oh! Right . . ." said Bryony, clearly taken aback.

Ellie's eyes widened in surprise at Isabelle's retort. Surely she couldn't have meant to sound so rude?

Sophie was laughing. "Oi—that's a bit of a cheek," she said, rolling her eyes to the rest of the girls. "You can't walk in here and say that to a bunch of Royal Ballet School students! *We* dance properly as well, thank you very much!"

Ellie waited for Isabelle to laugh, too, and confess that yes, she was only teasing and of course she was delighted to be studying at the prestigious Royal Ballet School.

But there was no trace of a laugh on Isabelle's lips. In fact, her expression couldn't have been more serious. She pulled off her other boot and slung it carelessly under her bed. "I can say what I like," she said crisply. Then she looked hard at Sophie. "As I'm sure you know, we French invented ballet. So if anybody knows the way to dance ballet properly, we do!"

Chapter 2

There was a stunned silence at Isabelle's pronouncement. Nobody knew what to say.

Isabelle unzipped her case. She obviously thought the conversation was quite over.

Ellie exchanged glances with Grace. Had Isabelle *really* just said all that? Grace's open mouth told Ellie that yes, she certainly had. Ellie couldn't help staring at Isabelle as she hung up her clothes neatly. Ellie would never have strode in like Isabelle, insult everybody in the room, and then carry on as if it were no big deal. Not in a billion years!

Every face said the same thing. Even talkative Sophie's mouth was still for once—lost for words as she, too, stared at this new girl who was confident to the point of being arrogant. Ellie's excitement at having a new face in the dorm was disappearing fast. Was Isabelle always like this? If so, how would the new girl ever fit in at The Royal Ballet School?

Ellie started to unpack her own clothes in the silence that had settled in the room. The other girls turned to their unpacking, casting glances Isabelle's way. Ellie really hoped that Isabelle was going to chill out and want to make friends with everybody. They did have to share a dorm together, after all!

Just then, the door opened, and in rushed Lara, closely followed by Kate.

"Hello, everybody!" they shouted in unison, wheeling their cases into the dorm. Ellie remembered they'd arranged to share a taxi from the airport. Lara was from Ireland, and Kate from Newcastle, a city in the far north of England.

Ellie ran over to greet them with the other girls. It was something of a relief, to have a distraction from Isabelle. But it didn't last long.

"Hello! Are you new?" Kate called, looking Isabelle over with great interest. "I'm Kate."

Isabelle looked up briefly from her unpacking. "Isabelle," was all she replied.

Kate opened her mouth to say something else, only to snap it shut again as Isabelle turned back to her clothes. Kate looked over at Ellie and the others, her eyebrows raised in surprise. They shrugged and Sophie pulled a funny face. Kate's lips twitched in amusement. "Well, charmed to meet you, Isabelle," she said rather sarcastically, and then made her way over to her end of the dorm with Holly and Rebecca.

Lara was watching with interest. "I didn't know we were getting a new girl!" she said, then lowered her voice. "What's she like?" she asked Ellie and Sophie. "She seems a tad frosty."

"Well, she . . ." Ellie began, and then stopped. After all, she'd only just met Isabelle. She knew herself just how hard it was to settle in to a new school in a foreign country, having moved from Chicago to England just over a year ago. Everybody had to find their own way, didn't they? Ellie was determined to give Isabelle a chance to be nice.

Sophie didn't have any such qualms about passing judgment. "Oh," she said airily to Lara, "she's just disappointed to be slumming it at The Royal Ballet School, that's all, having learned to dance in *la belle France*!"

Lara stared open-mouthed at Sophie. "Slumming it?" she echoed quietly.

Ellie could tell Lara was wondering whether the humorous glint in Sophie's eyes meant she was joking. "No joke," Ellie confirmed.

Lara raised her eyebrows. "Well, it looks like we're in for a fun term, then, doesn't it?" she said in a dry voice, low enough that Isabelle couldn't hear. "I can't wait for our first ballet class!"

"Fireworks, that's what I'm predicting," Sophie went on knowingly. "Great big explosive fireworks! In fact, my horoscope for today said that I should expect some confrontation. I guess Isabelle is it!"

Lara's green eyes gleamed. "I'd better go and introduce myself. Watch out for some sparks!"

She walked over to her bed, next to Isabelle's, and sat down on it. "Hello," she said conversationally. "I'm Lara, and I gather that you're Isabelle."

Isabelle was emptying her underwear into a drawer. Even that looked fancy, Ellie couldn't help noticing. "That's right," Isabelle replied, glancing over and coolly sizing Lara up with her dark eyes.

"So, we're going to be neighbors," Lara went on. "This is my bed here," she said, patting it affectionately. She leaned over in a conspiratorial way. "Sounds to me like you enjoy stirring things up, Isabelle. Didn't anyone tell you, that's *my* job?"

It was clear that Lara was joking, but Isabelle seemed to bristle at her words. "I am not here to stir anything up," she said haughtily, with another toss of her sleek, slippery-looking dark hair. "In fact, if I'd had any choice, I wouldn't be here at *all*. I would be in Paris, not . . ." She flung a hand out and looked witheringly around the room. "Not *here*."

The friendly smile vanished from Lara's face and her eyes flashed with a fierceness that Ellie knew always meant trouble. She'd been on the receiving end of that fierceness herself. She and Lara hadn't gotten along so well at first, but now they understood each other and were good friends.

"Well, maybe you should go *back* to Paris, then," Lara snapped back at Isabelle. "Because there's a queue of girls a mile long who'd take your place here at The Royal Ballet School in a second, you know."

Isabelle sniffed dismissively. "Well, *I* believe a *Paris* ballet school is the best place to be," she said, meeting Lara squarely in the eye.

Ellie braced herself for Lara's response. Irish Lara had a temper as fierce as her red hair. But just as Lara was opening her mouth to retaliate, Mrs. Hall reappeared in the dorm.

"Ah! You're all here now. Welcome back, everyone!" she said, with one of her wide, friendly smiles. "I thought I'd come to check that you've all settled back okay, before you rush off down to supper."

Ellie glanced up at the dorm clock in surprise. Time always went so fast in The Royal Ballet School—she couldn't believe it was suppertime already.

Mrs. Hall's gaze alighted on Isabelle. "This must all feel a little strange, Isabelle," she said sympathetically, "but I'm sure that everybody will do their best to help you feel at home here."

Isabelle gave a terse little nod in response, but said nothing.

"Well, we're *trying*," Ellie heard Sophie mutter. "But our best might not be good enough for Mademoiselle Armand," she added.

Mrs. Hall had sharp ears and turned at once in Sophie's direction, but Sophie promptly gave her a big, innocent smile. Mrs. Hall gave her a quizzical look, then carried on. "Anyway, I hope you've all had a good, restful Christmas break and have returned raring to go, ready to make the most of the new term. I'll be in the Slip later, if anybody needs to talk to me," she added. "Girls, could you show Isabelle where the canteen is, please?"

There was a rather awkward silence until Ellie hurriedly replied, "Yes, Mrs. Hall."

After their housemother had left the dorm, Lara vaulted over her bed toward Ellie. "Come on," she said. "Let's go and eat. I want to hear all about your holidays. I got your text message about *Swan Lake*. What was it like? Was it just gorgeous?"

"Gorgeousness itself," Ellie smiled. Then she called out to Isabelle. "Are you ready, Isabelle? We're going down to supper now."

Isabelle glanced up. "I am not hungry," she replied. "Besides, I would rather not go to dinner in my traveling clothes," she added, her eyes narrowing at the sight of Ellie and Lara in their jeans and sneakers.

Ellie bit her lip at the snub, not sure how to take the comment. Was Isabelle implying that she and Lara looked scruffy?

Lara put her hands on her hips. "Well, you put your ball gown on, Isabelle, and we'll see you later," she said frostily. "Come on, Ellie."

Ellie felt a little reluctant to leave Isabelle, having told Mrs. Hall that she'd take her down to supper. "If you're sure . . ." she said hesitantly, hovering at the end of her bed, as Lara, Sophie, and the others started going to the door.

Isabelle didn't bother looking up at Ellie. "That is what I said," she snapped.

"Okay," Ellie said, still feeling awkward at the idea of leaving the new girl alone on her first day at White Lodge. "Well . . . we won't be long. And I can always show you the canteen later if you want."

Isabelle didn't reply.

"Come *on*, Ellie, we're starving!" Sophie called out impatiently.

"Coming," Ellie replied, turning away from Isabelle. Well, she'd tried, hadn't she? She'd made an effort. But she couldn't *force* the new girl to come and eat with them, could she?

The tensions that had arrived with Isabelle were forgotten for a while as Ellie and her friends clattered through the Slip, the small room that connected the girls' dorm with the rest of the school, then down the huge stone staircase toward the canteen. Right now, there were far more important things to think about than Isabelle Armand—like being back at The Royal Ballet School!

●   ●   ●   ●

The next morning, Ellie woke a few minutes before Mrs. Hall was due to arrive with her cheery, "Good morning, girls, rise and shine!"

She lay there, smiling to herself. Oh, it was so exciting to be waking up at White Lodge again! She swung her legs out of bed and pulled on her dressing gown. To think she used to hate getting up in the morning when she'd attended regular school! Not here at The Royal Ballet School, though, where each day started with ballet class before regular academic classes. She could hardly wait for the day to begin!

"Ellie Brown, what on earth is that cheesy grin for?" Sophie called over sleepily from her bed. She yawned and stretched her arms above her head. "You look disgustingly cheerful for this time of the morning. Please stop it at once!"

Ellie laughed. It took Sophie a good half hour to perk up in the morning. "Just happy to be here with you, Soph, everybody's little ray of sunshine," she teased. "I can't help myself!"

Sophie pulled her pillow over her head. "I *am* a ray of sunshine . . . I *am* a ray of sunshine . . ." she chanted, making all the other girls giggle. "I . . . Oh, it's no good. I'm never going to be a morning person," she moaned.

Ellie, Bryony, Lara, and Grace exchanged knowing looks. Then, without another word, the four of them tiptoed up to Sophie's bed and, at a nod from Lara, whisked Sophie's quilt off her. "You ARE a ray of sunshine!" they chorused, laughing at Sophie's indignant squeals.

"And you'll be late, if you don't get a move on," Lara warned her. "Does your horoscope for today say anything about missing breakfast and being hungry all morning, sunshine?"

Sophie stopped squealing and sat up suddenly. "A school breakfast! Now, *that* is a good reason to get out of bed," she said, looking much happier. "The best meal of the day!"

Ellie agreed with Sophie on this. The canteen always served up a full English breakfast of bacon, eggs, sausages, mushrooms, baked beans, grilled tomatoes, and toast along with cereals, muffins, and croissants. Since the weather had grown cold, Ellie's favorite part of breakfast had become the school porridge, which was creamy and hot. Perfect for kick-starting a ballet dancer's body on a cold winter morning!

The girls all got dressed into their pink leotards, with their regulation red sweat suits and sneakers on top. All except Isabelle, who chose instead to pull on blue fleecy track pants and jacket over her pink leotard.

"I do not like red," she said, when she caught Ellie glancing curiously over at her.

"Yes, but everyone . . ." Ellie started. Then she closed her mouth. *Yes, but everyone wears the school sweat suit,* she wanted to say. *That's part of being here!* But she really didn't want an argument at seven-thirty in the morning. She'd let somebody else tell Isabelle, like Mrs. Hall. Instead, she turned and hurried after the others down to breakfast.

It seemed like the boys in Ellie's year were just as interested in the new student as the Year 7 girls were. As Isabelle entered the canteen, the group of boys in front of the cereal selection fell silent and watched her walk by. Then Ellie heard a wolf whistle.

"Very nice," Oliver Stafford said, smirking around at his friends. "This term is looking up already!"

Ellie rolled her eyes at Lara as they grabbed bowls of steaming porridge. *Well, wait until the boys actually* speak *to Isabelle Armand,* she thought to herself. *Then they might feel differently about her!*

*   *   *   *

After breakfast, the Year 7 girls went straight to their morning ballet class. Their teacher, Ms. Wells, was waiting for them in the studio. Her dark eyes sparkled as they all walked in. "Welcome back," she called cheerily. "Happy New Year, girls. It's very nice to see you again. I hope you've all been practicing *zealously* over the holiday!"

"Like my life depended on it, Ms. Wells," Sophie said mock seriously.

"Glad to hear it, Sophie," Ms. Wells chuckled. "Now, Bryony, Ellie, Lara, Megan, and Kate—I've heard wonderful comments about your *Nutcracker* performances over the Christmas season. I was so proud to see you doing such a splendid job. Well done."

Ellie and the others glowed with pleasure at her words. Ms. Wells wasn't the kind of person to dish out compliments unless she truly meant them. A word of approval from her was praise indeed!

Then Ms. Wells turned to Isabelle. "And welcome, Isabelle," she said with a friendly smile. "I remember seeing you audition last year. It's very nice to have you with us."

Isabelle, who had been leaning against one of the barres at the back of the studio, stepped forward slightly and curtseyed, but said nothing.

"Have you had a chance to get your uniform sorted out yet?" Ms. Wells asked her. "All our girls wear The Royal Ballet School's regulation red sweat suits."

Ellie watched Isabelle open her mouth to say something, and then shut it. Certainly she would have to wear red now!

"I hear you've come to us from Paris," Ms. Wells went on.

"Perhaps you could tell us all about your ballet training up to now?"

Isabelle looked a little taken aback to be asked, but then she quickly recovered herself. "I had my first ballet class when I was three years old," she began. "My teacher said I had a natural talent, and that I would go far with it."

Ellie tried not to look as startled as she was feeling inside at Isabelle's boastful words. Boy oh boy, Isabelle really did think she was something else!

"Last summer, I won the *prix national,* for young ballet dancers," Isabelle went on. "And I was chosen for the Paris Opéra Ballet School." She looked down at her feet. "It has always been my ambition to dance at the Paris Opéra one day. To me, it is the greatest ballet company in the world. *Alors . . .*" She shrugged. "I had to come to England instead, because . . ." She traced a pattern on the studio floor with her ballet shoe and then looked up, her eyes hard and proud once more. "Well, just because. So here I am."

"And we're just *thrilled* to have you," Sophie whispered sarcastically to Ellie.

Ellie couldn't help agreeing. Honestly! Isabelle was acting as if being at The Royal Ballet School was a comedown after her school in Paris. Talk about rude!

"Well, you never know," Ms. Wells said breezily, noting some of the eye rolling at the back of the class. "After a while here, maybe you will change your mind and aspire for a place in The

Royal Ballet instead!"

Ellie watched Isabelle's mouth form a disbelieving smirk that spoke volumes. *The Royal Ballet? Pah! What was The Royal Ballet compared to the Paris Opéra Ballet?* the smirk seemed to say.

The class began, as always, with some warm-up stretches and barre work. Ellie concentrated hard, loving the familiar pull in her hamstrings as she stretched over the barre, but she couldn't help the occasional glance over at Isabelle. And she quickly noticed she wasn't the only one sneaking looks at the French girl. The whole class was sizing her up as she went through the series of bends, stretches, and *pliés* Ms. Wells asked them to do. With all of Isabelle's bragging, there was no way she would get away without being thoroughly checked out by her fellow students!

It didn't take Ellie long to decide, rather ruefully, that Isabelle's talk hadn't actually been empty bragging. It was quite plain to even the most untutored eye that Isabelle Armand was superb. Better than superb. She was brilliant. Every movement flowed beautifully from one to the next. And, judging from the raised eyebrows around the class, Ellie wasn't the only person to think so.

"She is *so* good," Grace said gloomily, through gritted teeth, as they turned toward the barre for a series of *petits battements.* "*Too* good!"

Ellie patted her friend's hand comfortingly. Grace worried a lot and for absolutely no reason as far as Ellie could see. Grace was definitely one of the most accomplished dancers in their year, yet Ellie knew that she was sizing Isabelle up as a threat to her position. Even though Grace was modest, she always put pressure on herself to be the best. "Wait until we start on the floorwork, you'll knock the socks off her," Ellie whispered back.

A sigh escaped from Grace as she lifted her leg onto the higher of the two barres that ran around the room. She had two pink spots on her cheeks and her fair hair looked sweaty and disheveled. "I hope so," she muttered.

". . . and *battement tendu devant,*" Ms. Wells was saying. "Lead with the heel, that's it, Megan. Keep your back square, left arm to the side."

Ellie held her body in the familiar position, trying to keep her front knee straight as she stretched her front leg forward and pointed her toes.

"Don't break that wrist, Isabelle!" Ms. Wells called.

Ellie looked at Isabelle's outstretched arm and saw that her hand was hanging limply downward.

"At The Royal Ballet School, what we aim for is purity of line," Ms. Wells explained. "We hold the hand straight, fingers softly together, rather than having the wrist 'broken' so that the hand hangs." She demonstrated what she meant, elegantly extending her arm, hand straight and fingers softly together, to make the line as long and smooth as possible. "You see? Keeping the hand straight means that the line of the arm continues right to the tips of the fingers."

Isabelle stared at Ms. Wells's hand critically. "We do not care so much about such things in France," she said coolly, leaving her own hand exactly where it was.

Ellie and the other girls held their breath, *battements* forgotten, as they waited to see what was going to happen next. Nobody spoke to Ms. Wells that way!

Ms. Wells gave Isabelle a brisk smile, but there was also a glint in her eye. "I am aware of that, Isabelle," she said. "But we are not in France now, are we? We are at The Royal Ballet School in England. And purity of line is what The Royal Ballet style is all about."

Isabelle looked as if she wanted to stamp her foot, Ellie thought. She smothered a smile.

"But *I* am *French*, Madame," Isabelle replied haughtily.

Ms. Wells folded her arms across her chest. "We use a saying here in England, Isabelle," she said calmly, her eyes not leaving the new girl's face for a second. "When in Rome, I do as Rome does. And when you dance at The Royal Ballet School, you *dance The Royal Ballet School way.*"

Ellie had never heard Ms. Wells sound so stern. It was kind of scary, but also a little bit satisfying to hear Isabelle put in her place.

Isabelle tossed her head. And then, with an exaggerated movement, she straightened her hand, brought her fingers together and returned to the *battement.*

Everyone heaved a collective sigh of relief as the exercise continued.

Ms. Wells kept an eagle eye on Isabelle after that. A little later on, when they were all holding their arms above their heads in fifth position, Ms. Wells called out, "I can see spiky fingers!"

Ellie glanced over and saw that Isabelle's fingers were pointing spikily toward the ceiling. The rest of the class had their fingertips softly touching to form an arch over their heads.

Isabelle's mouth tightened sulkily as again Ms. Wells demonstrated The Royal Ballet School way to hold the position.

Ellie tensed, waiting for the new girl's rude reply, but Isabelle just sniffed in irritation and did as she was asked. Clearly she wasn't used to being corrected in ballet classes and was not happy about starting now!

●   ●   ●   ●

The rest of the day rushed by in a flurry of subjects. Ellie liked Mondays. After their morning ballet class, they had a math lesson with cheerful Mr. Best, then lunch, then geography, drama, and English lessons, followed by a break where they could have a snack from their tuck boxes. Afterward there was a character dancing class before supper and prep. Ellie particularly liked English with glamorous Ms. Swaisland, who somehow had a knack for making every book they read in class really interesting.

Like ballet class, Isabelle seemed very sure of herself in academic lessons. Ellie couldn't help but admire her, and hope that maybe Isabelle would begin to warm up to her new home. To start at a new school was one thing, but to start at a new school where every lesson was taught in your second language . . . Anybody else would have found it hard-going.

Ellie herself had experienced a few problems switching from American English to British English when she'd arrived in England from Chicago. Referring to "pants," which in England meant "underwear" and not "trousers," had caused the biggest hoot. And since then she'd discovered that many other words had slightly different meanings over here in England. She still tripped up sometimes. But at least the language was fundamentally the same one!

Isabelle had a much harder starting point, yet the French girl didn't seem to have any trouble following the lessons. Whenever Mr. Best asked the class for a solution to a math problem Isabelle was there, flinging up her hand with the correct answer. Even when Ms. Swaisland had them reading Shakespeare out loud, which usually had most of the class faltering over some of the language, Isabelle read fluently and expressively.

"She's a flipping robot," Sophie muttered as they trooped out of their English lesson and into the canteen for some much-needed tuck. "She's good at *everything*! I've been hoping all day she'd slip up at something, just so I'd feel better. Just to prove she's human! But—"

"Sssshhh," Ellie said warningly, spotting Isabelle coming into the dining area behind them.

"Well, you know what I mean," Sophie grumbled, foraging through her tuck box for a snack. She pulled out a candy bar and ripped it open with her teeth. "I wouldn't mind, but she's not even *nice* about it," she whispered as they watched as Isabelle inspected the drinks machine that provided hot chocolate and tea for the students.

A frown creased the new girl's forehead. "But where is the coffee?" she peevishly asked one of the canteen ladies.

The canteen lady smiled apologetically. "Sorry, love, we don't serve coffee," she replied. "Juice and water are much better for a dancer's body."

Isabelle's nose wrinkled in dismay. She sullenly helped herself to tea then sat down alone at a different table and glared at the cup as if it was to blame.

Bryony shook her head. "She's not exactly making it easy for herself, is she?" she commented, biting into a cereal bar.

"Not sitting there she isn't, anyway," Grace retorted. "That's the table where Oliver Stafford usually sits."

Ellie grinned. She didn't particularly like Oliver Stafford either. He was a bit bossy and arrogant. Some of the girls in Year 7 had a crush on him. Ellie could see he was good-looking, but boy, didn't he know it!

Isabelle sipped her tea and immediately pulled a face at the taste, peering disapprovingly into the cup.

"Ahh, let me guess, zee English tea is abominable," Lara said in an exaggerated French accent. "*Oh la la!* In France, we *always* 'ave coffee!"

Grace elbowed Ellie as Oliver Stafford moved away from his friends and strolled over to Isabelle, sitting next to her with a smile. "This might be interesting," she said.

"So . . . Isabelle, is it?" the girls heard Oliver ask as he held out a hand and smirked. "Oliver Stafford."

Isabelle looked rather disdainfully at Oliver's proffered hand, but didn't make any attempt to shake it.

"I've heard that you're French," he went on, pushing his floppy dark fringe out of his eyes and smiling engagingly. "My family went skiing in the French Alps just last week. Beautiful place."

"Yes," Isabelle said coolly, gazing past Oliver's shoulder as if she was barely aware that he was there.

A faint frown appeared on Oliver's forehead. *Clearly he's not used to being rebuffed*, Ellie thought to herself with a smile!

"So . . . er . . . welcome to The Royal Ballet School!" he finished, sweeping an arm around the room grandly, as if he owned it. "And I . . . um . . . look forward to getting to know you better, Isabelle."

Isabelle raised one eyebrow, rather witheringly, but said nothing.

Oliver finally took the hint—that she clearly wasn't interested!—and sloped back off to his friends.

Ellie couldn't help but grin, especially as Oliver's friends all started teasing him. "Isabelle's even snubbed Mr. I-Love-Myself-So-Much Stafford," Ellie said. "That's something in her favor, at least!"

Lara glanced at her watch, and then gulped down the rest of

her cup of tea. "Time for character class," she said, then lowered her voice. "Who wants to bet Mademoiselle Armand is *très bien* at that, as well?"

Sophie sighed and munched through her last mouthful of candy. "All bets are off," she said. "Let's face it—we all know she's going to dazzle everybody at character dancing, too. We'll just have to hope she gets partnered with Justin and his sweaty hands."

"Or Nick, who must be a good head shorter than she is," Bryony chuckled wickedly. "I can just see how she'd love that!"

Ellie giggled. "I don't think Oliver will be offering, do you?" she said. "Not now that he's been put in his place!"

Dear Diary,

I'm writing this in the common room, curled up in a corner of the sofa. Everyone else in here is watching a funny movie. Sophie keeps going on about how much she fancies a bag of popcorn. Mademoiselle Isabelle hasn't graced us with her presence, though.

I don't want to sound mean—I know how hard it is to be a new girl—but Isabelle is not exactly making it easy for anyone to like her. It's hard to imagine her having any friends at all, anywhere in the world, if she's always as rude as she is here! I nearly fell over after the way she answered Ms. Wells back in ballet this morning. No one, <u>no one</u>, speaks to the teachers like that! Thanks to Isabelle, this term certainly isn't going to be a dull one!

I just can't understand why Isabelle is being so mean! She's not even giving us a chance to be friends.

Chapter 3

"I can't wait to see what surprises Isabelle has lined up for us today," Lara muttered as they went to ballet class the following morning. "She'll probably pick a fight with the pianist this time. *In France, we do not play zee piano like zat. We know 'ow to play eet properly!*"

Sophie was practically rubbing her hands with glee. "Bring it on, Isabelle," she said. "Let the sideshow begin!"

Ellie grinned to herself as she slipped on her ballet shoes. Ballet lessons had never been boring at The Royal Ballet School, but she couldn't remember there ever having been an atmosphere of expectancy like there was today. Still, at least Isabelle was wearing her red sweat suit today—a better start than yesterday!

Ms. Wells clapped her hands for silence. "Good morning, everyone," she said crisply. "Let's warm up with some *pliés* first."

Ellie jumped at the tone of her teacher's voice. It was clear that she was expecting best behavior today!

As the class progressed through warm-up stretches, barre work, and center work, Ellie couldn't help glancing over at

Isabelle. She caught her friends doing the same and guessed that, like her, they were half-dreading yet half-hoping for a repeat performance of yesterday's fireworks. But Isabelle didn't seem to be looking for a fight today. She diligently remembered to hold her body in the unaffected Royal Ballet School style, like everybody else.

In fact, Ellie thought to herself, it was as if Isabelle had never danced any other way—which, Ellie had to admit, was pretty amazing.

"Who can tell me the three important stages of jumping?" Ms. Wells asked the class a little later.

A few hands shot up—including Isabelle's.

"Isabelle?" Ms. Wells asked.

"Entering a jump, holding a jump in the air, and completing a jump," Isabelle rattled off.

"Exactly," Ms. Wells replied. She looked pleased at Isabelle's succinct answer. "And don't forget: In every single stage of your jump, you must control the movement precisely. Let's begin!"

Ms. Wells drilled them on *temps levé*—a jump from one foot. "Point that foot underneath you . . ." She demonstrated, standing in fifth position with her shoulders slightly turned. "And long arms! The position of your arms and head must be exact. Now push yourself off! And *pas de chat! Pas de chat*!"

She then had the class line up to travel across the studio with the jump, one by one. "Remember, girls, spring *quickly* into the air each time."

Lara went first. Ellie watched as her friend stepped into her first *temps levé*, pushing herself nimbly into the air again and again until she reached the opposite corner of the studio.

"Good, Lara. Very nice . . ." Ms. Wells commented.

Lara, flushed and pleased-looking, relaxed against the barre.

Ellie gave her a thumbs-up. Lara was such a fantastic leaper, easily the best in the class.

"Isabelle, you next, please," said Ms. Wells.

Everyone watched with interest as Isabelle stood in fifth position. How would the new girl measure up to Lara's leaps?

"And away you go," Ms. Wells instructed.

There was silence in the studio, except for the shuffle and swish of Isabelle's footwork, soft and light as a cat.

Ellie watched critically. Isabelle's arms were long and graceful, her jump was high, and her *pas des chats* were crisp and clean. As she landed from her second *temps levé* with perfect balance, it was all Ellie could do not to gasp in admiration. When Isabelle jumped, Ellie could see exactly what Ms. Wells had meant about controlling every stage of the jump. Isabelle just seemed to hover mid-jump, frozen in position as if she were suspended from the ceiling, for far longer than gravity should have allowed. How did she manage it?

Isabelle's proud features softened slightly as Ms. Wells praised her. She'd seemed utterly lost in the movement, Ellie thought to herself. She'd even forgotten to scowl!

"Isabelle, I'm afraid you're going to have to go back to France,"

Sophie joked dryly from her place farther back in the queue, once Isabelle had finished. "You are just too good for my liking!"

Ellie and Bryony both chuckled, as did a few of the other girls, but there were some serious faces, too, Ellie noticed. Grace, in particular, looked a little tense. She was biting her lower lip, her face pale. Kate didn't look very pleased at Isabelle's performance, either.

Holly jumped next, then Bryony. When it was Grace's turn to cross the studio, she looked unusually flustered and began with the wrong foot in front.

"Other foot," Ms. Wells had to remind her. "Are you with us today, Grace?"

Grace's pale cheeks turned pink. "Yes, Ms. Wells," she replied. "Sorry."

Ellie watched her friend jump. Grace was a very good dancer, everybody knew that. Yet today she seemed rather rattled by the *temps levé*. Ellie knew that in ballet, you sometimes just had to trust your body with a movement, even if you weren't quite sure you could pull it off exactly right. She'd found in the past that getting too stressed about a difficult step often made things worse. It looked as if Grace was having that problem today, Ellie thought. She seemed so focused on getting the *temps levé* technically perfect that she looked robotic and miserable as she jumped across the studio.

Ellie willed her friend to relax and have faith that her body could do it. While Grace looked so anxious and tense, she was never going to achieve the fluid leaping motion that Lara and then Isabelle had demonstrated.

"Enjoy it, Grace, *enjoy* feeling yourself lift off from the floor," Ms. Wells urged her.

But Grace didn't seem to hear. She landed shakily after her *pas des chats* and slunk across to the other girls as if the step had truly beaten her.

Before Ellie could think about it any further, it was her turn to go. She took a deep breath and tried to enjoy the movement, as Ms. Wells had said, attempting to give as polished a performance as Isabelle had done. She felt a surge of exhilaration as she took off from the ground and, despite her concentration, she couldn't help smiling at the joyful experience of being in the air. It was the nearest thing to flying and it felt so wonderful!

"Good, Ellie," Ms. Wells said as she finished. "I'd like you to be a little more vertical while you're in mid-air, but other than that, very nice. It's good to see my dancers smiling!"

Ellie felt her cheeks flush with pleasure at her teacher's words and smoothed her leotard down happily. Who cared if Isabelle was supremely talented in the studio? It didn't mean that she, Ellie Brown, had to enjoy her ballet any less, did it? Soaring through the air had to be one of the greatest feelings in the world, and nobody but nobody would be able to take that away from her.

•   •   •   •

After ballet class, there was the usual rush as the girls showered and changed for their next lesson. When she'd first started at the Lower School, Ellie had found it hard to switch from an intensive, demanding ballet class to sitting behind a desk in a regular class in fifteen minutes. Now she was used to it, though, and as she pulled on her white school blouse and the blue/green plaid school skirt every morning, she was able to put ballet out of her head for the time being.

But Grace could not. As the pair of them raced down one of the long, low curving brick tunnels that led through the school, Ellie could hear Grace muttering to herself.

"And step and jump! Long arms. *Pas de chat, pas de chat.*"

"Grace, quit it," Ellie ordered her. "Just stop thinking about it now, and try again tomorrow. Sleep on it. Your feet will probably work it out all by themselves while you're dreaming."

"But I hate it when I can't do things straightaway," Grace grumbled as they made their way across the courtyard toward the computer block. A light drizzle was falling, and the girls shielded their heads with their folders as they ran over the rain-speckled cobblestones. "It just nags at me all day. I keep trying to get it right in my head."

"I know what you mean," Ellie sympathized as she pushed open the door to the computer studies classroom. "But, Grace, Mrs. Sanderson is going to go nuts if you keep muttering and tapping your feet for the next hour."

Grace gave her friend a weak smile as they sat down at neighboring computers. Then she let out a giggle. "What do you think she'll do if I start leaping over the desks, to get in some extra practice?" she asked.

Ellie glanced up at Mrs. Sanderson, who was ticking names off in her register as the students sat down. She leaned over to Grace. "I think she'll say, *Grace Tennant, what a SUPER temps levé!*" she whispered, in a high-pitched imitation of their teacher. Cheery Mrs. Sanderson seemed to think everything was "super."

"Morning, everybody," Mrs. Sanderson said at that moment. "I do hope you've all had a *super* Christmas break."

Ellie nudged Grace, and the pair of them collapsed into giggles, their shoulders shaking.

"Ellie Brown and Grace Tennant, what on earth is so amusing?" their teacher wanted to know.

It wasn't the greatest start to a computer studies lesson, but Ellie didn't mind too much. At least Grace was smiling again and that had to be worth the trouble.

· · · ·

It soon became apparent to everybody in the class that Isabelle knew her way around a computer as well as she did a ballet studio, even if she did keep sighing in annoyance and telling anybody who would listen how much better the computer system had been in her old school. And after lunch she showed that she was competent in the chemistry lab, too, as well as being knowledgeable in their history lesson—despite her disappointment that the syllabus didn't cover any *French* history.

"Is there *anything* that girl can't do?" Sophie groaned crossly as they made their way to the music room later that afternoon.

"It's starting to get me down. I wouldn't mind if she were a *friendly* genius, but she isn't. I hate the way she keeps looking down her nose at everybody, like she's some kind of superior being. D'you know, I'm starting to wonder if she's another Leo like me; she's such a show-off!" She sighed heavily and shook her head. "No, she can't be. Leos are sociable!"

"I hope she's tone deaf and won't be able to sing a note," Lara said, holding up crossed fingers as they pushed open the music room door.

Ellie elbowed her jokily. "Nothing wrong with being tone deaf, Lara McCloud," she said. "We can't all be musical maestros like you!"

Lara grinned at Ellie. "You're not tone deaf, Ellie," she said sweetly. "You just . . . sing all the notes in the wrong order. And in the wrong key. With the wrong tune. That's all. Apart from that, you have the voice of a nightingale!"

"The voice of a nightingale being attacked by a cat," Sophie teased. She, like Lara, was very gifted musically. While Lara played the piano and violin with great skill, Sophie had a wonderful singing voice. She often joked around with it, singing songs in funny voices or doing impressions of her favorite pop stars, but everybody knew that when she wanted to, Sophie could sing as clearly and sweetly as an angel.

"It's lucky I know that you two are only joking," Ellie said, pretending to be huffy. "Otherwise there could be some serious falling out, you guys."

Ms. Moulam, the music teacher, walked into the classroom just then, clutching a sheaf of music papers in one hand, and pushing up her spectacles with the other. As usual, her eyes peered around the class as if she was seeing them all for the first time. "Good afternoon," she said, dumping her pile of papers on the desk at the front of the room, and not seeming to notice when several of the top sheets drifted down onto the floor.

One of the boys sniggered—Oliver Stafford, it sounded like—but Ms. Moulam didn't appear to notice that, either. She looked around the room and then her eyes alighted on Isabelle, who stood up at once.

"Madame, I am a new student here," Isabelle said. "My name is Isabelle Armand."

Ms. Moulam scrabbled through her sheaf of papers for her register, sending a pen rolling off the desk. "Where has that blasted thing gone?" she mumbled to herself. "Ahh yes. Let's see . . . Isabelle. Right here. Marvelous. Do you play any instruments, Isabelle?"

"*Mais oui, Madame,*" Isabelle began in French, and then her olive cheeks blushed pink. "Yes, I mean," she said, with one of her shrugs. "Yes, of course. I am a ballerina, after all, Madame. Is it not crucial for a dancer to have musical ability?"

There were a few snorts from some of the less musical members of the class. Even Ms. Moulam looked amused. "You'd be surprised, Isabelle," she said dryly. "Some of the best dancers cannot play a note. The two things aren't inseparable. Obviously you need good rhythm, a good ear for a melody, some kind of ability to *interpret* a piece of music, but . . ." She also shrugged. "Unfortunately, as you will hear for yourself in this lesson, not all dancers are musicians, and vice versa."

"I bet they all are in France," Ellie heard Sophie whisper to Bryony.

Isabelle had a rather haughty look on her face. "I play the piano and violin," she announced proudly to Ms. Moulam. "I also play the clarinet."

Ellie sighed. Of course. Surprise, surprise! She should have known. Was there anything Isabelle Armand *couldn't* do?

•   •   •   •

That evening, after their weekly swimming lesson and supper, Ellie and her friends made their way down to play pool with Matt and some of the other Year 7 boys. The pool table was down in the logia, the open area that led out to the rear gardens. Matt had organized a match, boys against girls.

Sophie was just about to toss a coin to see who could start first when Ellie saw Isabelle heading toward one of the studios with her ballet shoes.

Matt had spotted her, too. "Hey, Isabelle, would you like to join in?" he invited.

Isabelle turned her head. "No, I would not," she replied with a slight shudder.

It was, Ellie thought irritably, as if Matt had just asked her if she wanted to eat a dead spider.

Matt looked rather taken aback at the bluntness of Isabelle's tone, and tried to shrug it off. "Um . . . okay, then," he said.

Ellie felt sorry for Matt. He was such a friendly person—he was only trying to make the new girl feel at home. Why did Isabelle have to throw the offer back in his face that way?

Sophie flipped the coin and slapped her hand over the top of it. "Don't tell me you're going to do more ballet practice, are you, Isabelle?" she asked, with a grin. "You're going to show us all up at this rate!"

It was obvious to everybody that Sophie was only joking, but Isabelle just raised her eyebrows and said haughtily, "I thought I already did that this morning."

Sophie's mouth shut with a snap. She was so shocked, she let go of the coin and it bounced under the pool table. For once, Sophie didn't have a snappy comeback.

Lara did. "You wish!" she bellowed after Isabelle's retreating back. "Rude cow!" she growled. "Why didn't she just stay in France? Didn't they want her, either?"

Unfortunately for Lara, Mr. Barrington happened to be strolling by and heard Lara's angry remark. "You should be making an effort to help Isabelle settle in, not calling her names," he said crossly. "I thought better of you, Lara McCloud. Don't let me hear you say anything like that again!"

Lara's face was like a thunderstorm as Mr. Barrington walked away. "That Isabelle!" she grumbled to Ellie. "Now she's gone and gotten me into trouble! Thanks very much, *Mademoiselle Armand*!"

Ellie didn't know what to say—they *were* making an effort, but Isabelle didn't even attempt to be nice.

Ellie got down on her hands and knees and felt around under the pool table for Sophie's coin. "Let's just ignore her," she said, fishing it out and dusting it off. She flipped the coin up and covered it as Matt called out, "Heads!"

Ellie uncovered the coin to show tails. "Excellent," she said. "Now, are we girls gonna humiliate the guys or *what?*"

"You bet!" Sophie cheered, chalking up a cue. Lara remained silent, her green eyes still glaring after Isabelle.

Ellie sighed and squeezed Lara's hand. Isabelle Armand was really getting to everybody!

Dear Diary,

I'm writing this snuggled up in bed. It's f-f-f-freezing outside tonight! It makes me think about winter in Chicago. I wonder if it's snowing back there? Heather and the rest of my old gang will be having sled races and snowball fights every day. Must e-mail Heather tomorrow.

It's been another weird day at school, because of Isabelle. It's like she's really __mad__ that she's here, instead of feeling like the rest of us do, that it's the most awesome honor in the world. I've never known anybody who is so breathtakingly RUDE all the time!

Yesterday in ballet class she made that comment about having to come here "because . . . well, just because." It's made me wonder—because what?? Just why IS she here?

"Finally! A proper bundle of post for us girls!"

Ellie smiled at Sophie, who was waving the pile of mail in the air with a triumphant grin. The Year 7 girls had just come from their morning ballet class and had stopped by the canteen to see if any mail was waiting for them. The students' mail was usually sorted and left in the canteen for them by mid-morning, and Ellie always looked forward to seeing if she'd been sent anything.

Lara, as was often the case, had several things to open. She and Sophie got the most letters from friends at home, largely because they were both very good at writing back to people. Grace had a parcel from her mom, and Ellie pounced on a postcard from Chicago with Heather's handwriting on it.

Hi, Ell, she read on the way back up to the dorm.

Hope school is cool. We've had a ton of snow this week. Libby and I went sledding down Montgomery Hill, black ice all the way! She and Ruthie say hi. Mom's taking me to the Bears game this weekend. Can't wait! Write soon! Tons of love, Heather x x x

Ellie flipped over the postcard and gazed at a picture of the Cloud Gate sculpture in Chicago's Millennium Park, where she'd loved to hang out with her friends. She had a sudden memory of herself and Heather Rollerblading along together, stopping for a corn dog and a soda, getting the El train home . . . She felt a rush of nostalgia for her old life in the U.S.

Once they were in the dorm, Grace started ripping open her parcel. "My *hair clips*!" she exclaimed thankfully, pulling them out. "I can't believe I left them at home. Now I can stop borrowing yours all the time, Ell."

The girls crowded around Grace as she emptied the rest of her parcel. "Warm socks—thank goodness," she said, pulling them out of the box and waving them triumphantly. "My toes were freezing last night. What else? Oh, cool, my CDs!"

The only person who wasn't interested was Isabelle. She was blow-drying her wet hair after her shower. Now that she thought about it, Ellie couldn't remember Isabelle receiving *any* mail yet, not even a postcard. Neither had she had any phone calls or text messages, as far as Ellie knew. *Did Isabelle even have a cell phone?* she wondered.

Ellie glanced at her watch and then grabbed her things for the shower. If she didn't get a move on, she'd be late for her biology lesson! She gave one last look at her postcard, and then flew to the shower room to get washed and changed.

•   •   •   •

In French class that afternoon, Ms. Blanchard wanted everyone to say something in French about his or her family or home. She gazed around the room, and Ellie dropped her eyes quickly. She didn't want to get picked to go first!

"Bryony," Ms. Blanchard said. "Tell us about your mother. What does she look like?"

Bryony thought for a second then began haltingly, *"Ma maman a des cheveux noirs . . . et des yeux bruns . . ."*

"Très bien," Ms. Blanchard smiled. *"Et votre papa?"*

"Mon papa a des cheveux bleus . . . et des yeux rouges," Bryony replied.

Isabelle gave a snort of amusement. "Your father has *blue hair* and *red eyes*?" she translated.

Ms. Blanchard shot Isabelle a little frown.

Bryony flushed. "Red hair and blue eyes, I meant!" she said. *"Cheveux rouges et yeux bleus."*

"Merci, Bryony," Ms. Blanchard said, writing *cheveux rouges* and *yeux bleus* on the blackboard. "Who's next? Isabelle. We already know you're from Paris, you lucky girl! But what is your home like?"

For once, Isabelle looked a little disconcerted. There was a pause of several moments before she began to reply in quick, fluent French.

Ellie strained her ears, hoping to pick out something that would tell her more about the new girl. *". . . Maman habite à Paris . . ."* she picked up. And then, *"Mon père habite à New York maintenant . . ."*

Ellie's eyes widened. Had Isabelle just said that her mom lived in Paris, but her dad lived in New York? She gazed thoughtfully at Isabelle. Having parents on two different continents couldn't be much fun, even for somebody as self-confident and independent as Isabelle.

Ms. Blanchard asked Isabelle another question in French, but Ellie didn't catch what it was because she was too busy thinking about what Isabelle had just said. And she stood no chance of understanding the rapid-fire French answer Isabelle gave. It was so frustrating!

After the lesson ended, Ellie watched as Isabelle picked up her textbooks and went off on her own for tuck in the canteen. She nudged Lara. "Did you hear what Isabelle said to Ms. Blanchard?" she asked.

Lara gave a snort. "I switch off whenever Isabelle opens her mouth," she replied. "It's always me, me, me with her. Or rather, *moi, moi, moi.*"

Ellie told Lara what she'd heard—or thought she'd heard—as they followed the others down to the canteen.

Lara shook her head and looked rather guilty for being so scornful earlier. "I had no idea. That must be hard," she said sympathetically.

As they entered the canteen, they saw Isabelle sitting alone as usual.

"Come on," Lara said as she collected her tuck box from the shelf. "Let's go and make an effort."

Ellie took her own tuck box and followed Lara over to Isabelle's table.

"Hi," Lara began conversationally, sitting down opposite Isabelle. "Mind if we join you?"

Isabelle looked up from the bar of French chocolate she was carefully breaking open. "You are free to do as you like," she said dismissively.

There was an awkward silence for a few moments, and then Lara began, "It must be nice for you, being able to speak French with Ms. Blanchard," she said, stirring her tea.

"Yes," Isabelle replied. She sipped her hot chocolate. *"C'est la belle langue;* it is the most beautiful language. I miss speaking French."

Ellie took a deep breath. "Did I hear you say that your dad lives in New York, Isabelle?" she asked.

Isabelle looked faintly uncomfortable at the question. "He moved there from Paris last year," she confirmed.

Just then, Sophie came and sat down at the table, looking curiously at Ellie and Lara. "Thought I'd come and see what's so interesting about this table," she joked, ripping open a candy bar and taking an enormous bite.

"So, Isabelle," Lara went on, "if you don't mind me asking, why *are* you at school in England rather than in Paris?"

Two red spots appeared on Isabelle's cheeks. "My mother is no longer happy in Paris," she said tersely. "She is planning to move back here, and decided that I must come here, too."

"Move *back*?" Ellie blurted out, surprised.

Isabelle gave a stiff little nod. "My mother grew up here before moving to Paris to study art."

Sophie crumpled up her already empty candy wrapper. "I see! So you're half-*English*, Isabelle," she said, unable to hide her delight. Then she put on a sorrowful expression. "It must be a terrible embarrassment. How can you possibly *live* with yourself?"

Isabelle's mouth tightened. She was clearly angry at Sophie's teasing, and got up to leave.

Ellie half-wished that Sophie hadn't come along just then. Maybe Isabelle would have told them more about herself. Clearly there were a lot of changes happening in her life. Her family was no longer together, which is difficult for anyone, but why wouldn't she want to be part of The Royal Ballet School family?

• • • •

The next morning in ballet class, Ms. Wells gathered the girls in front of her before they warmed up. "Good morning, everyone," she said. "Now, I don't want to put a dampener on your good moods, but I've been asked to remind you all that the ballet appraisals take place next month, just before half-term."

"Like we needed reminding," Grace muttered to Ellie, looking sick at the thought.

"It'll be fine, Grace," Ellie whispered back. But she, too, felt a twinge of anxiety at the thought.

"Could you please explain these *appraisals*?" Isabelle asked Ms.

Wells. "I have not heard of them. Are they like an examination?"

"Oh, sorry, Isabelle," Ms. Wells apologized. "Of course you won't have heard about the appraisals yet. Yes, they are an examination of sorts. You will be asked to perform a series of rehearsed routines in front of Lynette Shelton, our School Director, and a panel of assessors," she explained. "The assessment results are posted to you during the half-term vacation."

"Oh," said Isabelle. "That is all? I am always good at examinations."

"Glad to hear it," Ms. Wells replied, sounding amused.

Sophie rolled her eyes at Ellie.

Ellie knew that all her friends were thinking about what Ms. Wells hadn't said: that if you didn't make the grade, there were no second chances. You would have to leave the school at the end of the year. Not everyone was destined to be a ballerina.

Ms. Wells glanced around at the solemn faces in front of her and gave an encouraging smile. "Please try not to worry," she said. "The appraisal is mainly a process to help you with the progress of your ballet. It's very rare for a student to be appraised out of The Royal Ballet School in Year 7. Just keep practicing and doing your best."

Ellie forced a smile, but she couldn't help but imagine how terrible it would feel to have to leave The Royal Ballet School at the end of the year. It was just about the most horrible thing she could think of.

That day's class began. Ellie gritted her teeth and knuckled down to the exercises, determined to work extra hard from now on!

After the girls had warmed up and worked at the barre and in the center of the studio, Ms. Wells had them change into their pointe shoes.

As usual, pointe work started with a few slow rises at the barre to warm the muscles in their feet.

"Lift off those toes!" Ms. Wells called as Ellie and the other girls raised the balls of their feet off the floor. "No scrunching them up!"

Next, they began a series of *échappés en pointe*. "*Demi-plié* in fifth," Ms. Wells instructed them, "then spring onto pointe in second."

Ellie performed the movement, remembering to keep her knees pulled up and the weight balanced over both feet as she went up onto her toes. It still gave her such a thrill, being *en pointe*. It really made her feel like a true ballerina!

"And . . . back to *demi-plié* in fifth," Ms. Wells said. "Very nice."

After a few more *échappés*, Ms. Wells announced that they were going to learn a new movement *en pointe*. "This is called *pas de bourrée piqué*," she told them, "and, before anybody asks, yes, this is going to be one of the routines in the appraisals."

A nervous buzz went around the studio. Ellie's tummy tightened at the words.

"We'll start off at the barre," Ms. Wells told them, "and then, when you're used to the movement, we'll take it into the center."

Ellie watched as her teacher nimbly demonstrated the new step. Ms. Wells always seemed to make ballet look effortless—but Ellie wasn't fooled for a second. She could see that the *pas de bourrée piqué* would be quite tricky.

"Start in fifth," Ms. Wells said, going through the movement more slowly this time, "then pick up the back foot into *coup de pied*, and step up onto it like so. Then your other leg needs to come up under the knee—everybody see?"

Ellie and the other students nodded.

"And then that foot steps to the side away from the body," Ms. Wells went on. "You need to transfer the weight from the supporting leg onto the stepped leg. Then, the other leg comes up under the knee. Pick up, step. Pick up, close . . . see?"

Ellie bit her lip. So far, in their pointe work, they had been balancing on *both* feet, which made life a little easier. But with the "pick up" that Ms. Wells had shown them, the weight was all transferred onto one foot, *en pointe*. She hoped her balance would be strong enough to support her!

"Now it's your turn to try," Ms. Wells said. "Start in fifth, girls."

They went slowly through the movement. "And . . . pick up," Ms. Wells instructed.

Ellie took a quick breath and picked up her left leg, but she felt so unsteady that she promptly put it straight back down again, clutching onto the barre for support. "Whoops," she said, feeling self-conscious. She wasn't the only one to have both feet on the ground, though. Sophie had done exactly the same thing and Rebecca had, too.

"Step to the side, and pick up," Ms. Wells was instructing the other girls.

Ellie gave her foot a wiggle, watching Lara as she managed the new step. And there, too, was Isabelle performing it faultlessly! A flush of pleasure had spread across the new girl's face. She really did love her ballet, Ellie thought to herself. In fact, she seemed a different person when she was dancing—she almost seemed like one of them, just a regular girl who loved to dance, instead of the proud outsider she was the rest of the time.

Ellie sighed and prepared to try the new step again. She remembered Grace struggling with *temps levé* in class the day before and reminded herself that, in ballet, sometimes you just had to trust your body. But Ellie *hadn't* trusted her foot to hold her up just now.

"Let's all try again," Ms. Wells said, walking over to Ellie. "Off we go. And . . . pick up, Ellie!"

Ellie took a deep breath. She could feel her tension running right through to her toes. She lifted her left leg again. This time she overbalanced, stumbling over to her right.

Her cheeks burned—Ms. Wells had seen her really mess up the step. She hated feeling as if she couldn't get a step right, but it was even worse to do it right under her teacher's nose.

"You're throwing your weight back, Ellie," Ms. Wells told her. "Try again, with your weight forward and over your toes."

Ellie bit her lip and tried to concentrate extra-hard. Then she attempted the movement again under her teacher's watchful gaze, but the same thing happened. What was she doing wrong? Why couldn't she balance, like everybody else? She tried again and again, but she still couldn't get the movement right. A churning feeling started up in her tummy. Hadn't Ms. Wells said that this was going to be part of the appraisal routine? She had to get it right! She just had to!

Ms. Wells must have seen Ellie's face scrunched up in frustration. She placed a comforting hand on Ellie's shoulder. "You'll get it," she said. "I promise. It's just something new, that's all. Your body will work it out." Then she addressed the rest of the class. "I think that's enough on pointe for today," she said. "We'll try that step in the center another time. Now, let's do some cool-down stretches before we finish for the morning."

Ellie felt glum as she and the rest of the class stretched out their tired muscles. Why hadn't she been able to do the new step? Rebecca had managed it after a few tries, and Sophie, too. She'd been the only one in the class who hadn't been able to get it right.

She rested her hot cheek on the barre as they stretched out their hamstrings. She couldn't understand what had gone wrong. She'd loved all the pointe work they'd done so far—from the excitement of learning how to tie the ribbons of her pointe shoes around her ankles to that magical first time she'd lifted off the ground and stood on the ends of her toes. Sure, there had been the initial discomfort of breaking in the new pointe shoes, so stiff and unyielding for the first few classes. But that problem hadn't taken long to resolve itself, and, before long, her pointe shoes had come to feel soft and pliable. It was as if they were a second skin around her feet.

Ellie jumped when she realized that the class was giving its *reverence*. She hurried to join in the curtseyed thanks to Ms. Wells and the pianist, and then followed the others to the side of the studio to pull on her sweat suit.

"Don't worry about it," Bryony said kindly as the girls collected their ballet bags. "Tomorrow you'll be pirouetting on pointe in the center, I bet you!" she joked.

Ellie gave a weak smile. "At the moment, I can't imagine ever being able to do that in a hundred years!" she said.

"In a hundred years, you'll be too old anyway," Sophie commented, trying to lighten Ellie's mood. "I can just see you, in your support tights with a walking stick . . . and a lovely beige polyester leotard!"

Lara snorted with amusement. "What a gorgeous image," she chuckled, pushing open the studio door. "Sophie, you really know how to cheer a girl up!"

Ellie laughed with the others, but inside, she couldn't stop running through the *pas de bourrée piqué* again and again. *Oh, please let me be able to get it right tomorrow,* she wished fervently as she followed them out of the studio. *Please!*

·   ·   ·   ·

The arrival of a chatty letter from her friend Phoebe with some photos of the two of them in Oxford lifted Ellie's spirits slightly. And the usual busy routine of academic lessons just about managed to distract Ellie from her morning disaster.

Later that evening in the common room, Ellie noticed that Grace was a little quieter than usual. "You okay?" she asked.

Grace jumped at Ellie's words, as if she'd been in a world of her own. "Fine," she replied quickly. Then she frowned. "Not really," she admitted. "It's all this talk of appraisals," she sighed. She looked around to check that nobody was listening. "I can't help thinking that, now that Isabelle's here and is so utterly brilliant at ballet, it's going to lower my grade in comparison."

Ellie frowned. "Is that how it works?" she asked.

Just then, Jessica Walters walked into the common room. Jessica was Ellie's guide from Year 8 and had been assigned to help Ellie with any problems she came up against.

Ellie waved her over. "Hey, Jessica," she asked, "is it true that in the appraisals, if somebody is ultra-fantastic, the other students get marked down by comparison?"

Jessica shook her head and sat down on the arm of the sofa Ellie and Grace were sitting on. "No, it's not a competition," she told them. "You all get marked on your own merits, regardless of any—what did you call them?—ultra-fantastic dancers there might be in the class. The appraisals can be really helpful in showing you what you need to work on." She gave a sympathetic smile at their glum faces. "Honestly, I swear it's not a big deal. I know it's scary. We all thought so last year, too, but afterwards you will wonder what all the fuss was about. Promise!"

"Was anybody appraised out of Year 7 last year?" Grace wanted to know.

"No," Jessica replied. "Nor the year before."

"Just do your best," Carli, another Year 8 girl, told them. "Everyone is here because they deserve to be! There'd have to be a *really* good reason for anyone to get appraised out. It's sooo not likely to happen."

Dear Diary,

Today wasn't the greatest day I've ever had at The Royal Ballet School. First of all, Ms. Wells hit us with the reminder of appraisals—ugh—and THEN she taught us a really tricky new step, pas de bourrée piqué, that I just could not do! Now I'm freaked out about it, because I know that's going to be part of the assessment. I've just GOT to get it right before then!

Everybody discussed the appraisals in the common room tonight. It seems like most of us have something we are worried about. Grace was still fretting about her temps levé after messing that up the other day, and Lara isn't looking forward to the port de bras section of the appraisal. Only Isabelle seems unruffled. "Oh, that is okay. I am good at examinations," she said. Honestly, she is so full of herself! Still, yesterday at lunch Isabelle seemed to open up a little bit. It must be hard having her parents living in different places. But why does she have to take it out on everybody else?

Grace is getting a little stressed out about Isabelle, too. She's worried that because Isabelle is so brilliant, it'll mean her grades will suffer by comparison. Jessica told us that it's not a competition, but Grace didn't seem too reassured. Poor Grace. I think it is mostly because her mom really wants Grace to be the best.

Jessica said that the appraisals are supposed to help us and that hardly anybody gets assessed out. She said to do my best, and I always try. But what if the appraisal comes and I still can't do the pointe work?

"Ellie—Ellie! Are you awake?"

Ellie rolled over in bed and opened her eyes to see Lara leaning over her, green eyes sparkling with excitement.

"I am now," Ellie mumbled, still half-asleep. "But it's Saturday morning . . . why are you up so early?"

"Come and see, come and see!" Lara whispered, pulling the nearby curtain aside. "Look!"

Ellie dragged herself out of bed, rubbing her eyes groggily. She padded over to stand by the window with Lara. Then, suddenly, she was as wide awake as her friend. "Snow!" she cried in delight. Snowflakes were twirling past the window, landing on the window ledge right under their noses.

"Isn't it wonderful?" Lara exclaimed as they both stared out at the whitened grounds and parkland beyond. The drive in front of the school was completely white, its circular shape marked only by the staff cars parked on it, which were now indistinguishable white mounds. The stark branches of the bare winter trees were sagging under the weight of their snowy coating.

"Whoopee!" Ellie cried, louder than she'd meant to. "BIG

snowball fight today, I reckon!"

Grace and Sophie were stirring now, and Isabelle.

"It's snowing, it's snowing!" Ellie told them excitedly.

Grace blinked and lifted her head off the pillow. "I hope the roads will be okay," she said immediately. "Mum's coming to get me this morning."

Bryony was awake now, too. "And I'm catching a train to my grandma's," she said, with a yawn. "I hope the trains are all still running."

"Look, there's Mr. Cartwright," Lara said, catching sight of the school caretaker. "He's putting salt down on the driveway. Don't worry, girls, you'll still get your weekends away."

Watching Mr. Cartwright, Ellie couldn't help feeling a teeny bit disappointed that all the snow was going to be cleared. There was something exciting about the thought of the whole school being snowed in together, completely cut off from the rest of the world. She could easily imagine it happening back in the eighteenth century, when White Lodge was a hunting lodge for the King of England. In the middle of enormous Richmond Park, it sometimes really did feel as if they lived miles from anywhere.

•　　　•　　　•　　　•

After the girls got dressed, Grace's mom arrived, although the snowy roads made her later than expected, and the school minibus took Bryony to Richmond train station to go to her grandmother's house. Holly, Scarlett, and Alice were all going home for the weekend, too.

"Who's coming for a snowball fight, then?" Sophie asked the others.

Everyone was excited about the idea—except for Isabelle. "I prefer to go for a walk," she said, zipping up her boots, then wrapping a thick coffee-colored scarf around the collar of her suede coat.

"That's a shame," Sophie joked, when Isabelle had left the dorm. "I was hoping for a good excuse to throw something at her."

Outside, Matt and some of the other Year 7 boys were already rolling snow into snowballs and hurling them at one another.

"Girls against boys!" Ellie shouted, lobbing a snowball straight at Matt's head.

He looked stunned as it landed right on his woolen hat. Then he spotted Ellie giggling behind her gloves. "Ellie Brown, I might have known," he said, mock severely. "I hope you realize you're going to regret throwing that!" He scooped up a handful of snow, patted it roughly into shape, and chucked it straight in Ellie's direction.

Ellie ducked down neatly, only for the snowball to splat onto Sophie's shoulder.

"Right, Matt Haslum!" Sophie yelled. "You've done it now. This is WAR!"

Within minutes everybody was rolling snowballs and throwing them as hard as they could, while trying to dodge the flying white missiles coming back at them. Before long, Ellie and her friends were red-cheeked and breathless, and covered with snow.

Ellie laughed as she watched Lara and Kate rugby-tackle Oliver and bring him to the ground, while they stuffed handfuls of snow down his neck.

He scooped snow blindly over his shoulder at them, in great white sparkling sprays. "Get off!" he yelled.

"You've RUINED his hair now, girls," Ellie laughed. "And we all know that took him ages to style this m—"

WHAM! A snowball walloped straight into her chest before she could finish her sentence. Matt again. He was *so* asking for trouble!

SPLAT! SPLAT! She pelted him with a double whammer: one snowball in each hand. But her aim was so wild, they both landed way over his head.

Breathlessly, she turned to get fresh snow. And as she did so, she saw Isabelle walking in the distance, keeping well out of the way.

Ellie stood up and waved both hands above her head. "Isabelle!" she hollered. "Come and help us get the boys!"

Isabelle looked over in Ellie's direction, and Ellie was sure she saw a tiny smile flicker on Isabelle's lips at the sight of Oliver all covered in snow. She watched as Isabelle hesitated, looking torn.

Then Isabelle shook her head. "I don't want to get snow on my coat," she called back. "It will mark the suede. Maybe—"

SPLAT! A snowball landed right into Ellie's face and she jumped back, gasping in shock. The rest of Isabelle's sentence was lost to her as she wiped snow off her cheeks and eyelashes.

When she looked back to where Isabelle had been standing, there was an empty space. Ellie couldn't help feeling a little disappointed. Just for a second, she'd been sure that Isabelle was going to loosen up, enjoy herself, and join in.

But no. The moment had been lost.

It wasn't long before someone suggested they call off the fight and go to the canteen for hot chocolate. Ellie cheered out loud, suddenly realizing just how cold and wet she was. Hot chocolate and dry clothes suddenly seemed like the best idea she'd heard for ages!

•   •   •   •

Later that afternoon, the snow had started to fall again and a bitter wind swirled around the school, rattling the large Georgian windows. Nobody wanted to play outside anymore.

While Sophie went off to write some e-mails, Ellie and Lara went to practice their *sissonnes* together in the Salon. Ellie wished she could practice her pointe work, but she knew unsupervised pointe work was strictly forbidden. If something went wrong when she was *en pointe*, she could mess up her whole ballet career!

The clouds outside were so thick and heavy, they had to switch on the overhead lights.

"Wow, you can hardly see a thing out there," Ellie said, wiping her hair out of her eyes after they'd been jumping for half an hour or so.

She and Lara gazed out of the long windows that reached up

to the high Georgian ceiling. Snowflakes were buffeting against the glass, a dizzying, tumbling eddy of white that was piling up ever higher outside. From this studio, it was usually possible to see beyond the school grounds and far into Richmond Park. On a clear day, you could even glimpse some of the taller buildings in central London. But today, they could barely see ten feet past the window.

"Phew! I'm glad we're not out there now," said Lara.

Ellie nodded, shivering at the very sight of the wintry scene on the other side of the glass. "It's like a horror movie: us in the middle of nowhere, in an old house, in a raging storm. Any minute now, the electricity will be cut, and we'll see spooky faces at the window. Vampires and . . ."

"Come on," said Lara, bringing her attention back to the warm studio. "This is London, not Sleepy Hollow. Let's do one more set each."

*   *   *   *

Back in the dorm a little later, they found Sophie, Kate, and a couple of the others snuggled up on their beds, chatting. The snow had picked up even more; now it was a constant flurry of white outside the window.

"You should have come with us," Ellie said, peeling off her sweaty leotard. "Half an hour of jumping, and my body thinks it's a summer day!"

Sophie gave a huge, dramatic sigh. "But it's the weekend," she said. "You're both nuts! The only thing I'm going to get out of bed for is—"

"Lunch!" Megan suddenly announced, looking up at the dorm wall clock.

Sophie immediately leapt off her bed. "Correct!" she laughed. "Perfect timing, Megan!"

•   •   •   •

While everyone was eating, the housemothers came in and began counting their students. "Nobody is to go outside in this snow," Mrs. Hall told the Year 7 girls. "It's too wild out there now. You're all to stay inside for the rest of the day and keep warm. Now, have we got everybody?"

Ellie looked around. There was herself, of course, Lara, Sophie, Megan, Rebecca, Kate . . . but no Isabelle, she realized. "Mrs. Hall? Isabelle isn't here," she called.

"Has anybody seen Isabelle Armand?" Mrs. Hall asked around the canteen.

"She was around this morning," Ellie said, trying to think when she'd last seen her. "She was walking around outside while we had our snowball fight."

"Has *anybody* seen her since then?" Mrs. Hall asked.

Nobody had.

Mrs. Hall was now looking very serious. "I hope she hasn't wandered off on her own outside the school grounds," she said. "She has been told that Richmond Park and beyond is out of bounds to unaccompanied Year 7 students. Did she mention going out to anyone?"

Ellie and her friends shook their heads. They'd barely spoken to Isabelle that day, let alone talk to her about her weekend plans. And as for reminding her of the school rules . . . *Like any of us would dare!* Ellie thought to herself.

Mrs. Hall glanced anxiously at the gloomy sky outside. "On a day like today, it'll start getting dark in a couple of hours," she observed, turning to the other housemothers. "I've got a student missing," she called. "Isabelle Armand. She's probably inside somewhere, but it's better to be safe than sorry. It would be easy for anybody to lose their bearings outside in this weather, let alone somebody who's new to the school. We'd better organize a search."

Some of the older students who had remained at school for the weekend offered to search the grounds while the Year 7s and 8s searched the school building.

"I don't think Isabelle would have stayed outside once the weather got so nasty," Lara pointed out as everyone hurriedly stacked their trays and sorted themselves into groups. "She wouldn't have wanted to get snow on that posh coat of hers, would she?"

"True," Ellie and the others agreed.

Ellie, Lara, and Sophie set off to search together. They decided they should check the dorm first, in case Isabelle had chosen not to have lunch and had returned to the dorm when everyone else was in the canteen.

But the dorm was empty, and so were the Slip and the common room. They checked the studios, but they were all deserted. She wasn't in the computer block sending e-mails either, or swimming in the indoor pool.

"This is starting to give me the creeps," Ellie said. She couldn't help wincing every time the wind battered against the school building. The storm was getting worse by the minute. If Isabelle was lost outside, she was going to be freezing cold by now, expensive coat or not. "Where can she *be*?"

"I'm running out of ideas, too," said Lara. "The library?"

"It's worth a go," said Sophie, and they raced back along the tunnel to the school library that was tucked away at the far end.

Curled up in a comfortable library chair, nose in a book, and looking very cozy indeed, was . . .

"Isabelle! You're here!" Ellie cried in relief.

Isabelle looked up as she turned a page of her novel. "Yes, I am here," she said, sounding rather astonished that anybody should care. "Why are you looking for me?"

"Nobody's allowed to go outside. Mrs. Hall said so," Ellie told her, the words coming out in a rush. "You weren't at lunch, and we were worried you were outside . . ."

"We thought you might have gotten lost," Sophie chimed in.

"We thought you might have gone into the park," Lara added.

Isabelle looked out at the dark sky. "Go out? Into the *park*?" she repeated incredulously. "Why would I go out in this terrible English weather? Do you think I am crazy?"

"No," Ellie said lamely. "But . . . well, we didn't know whether you'd remembered that we aren't allowed in the park on our own . . . that's all."

Isabelle shrugged. "Of course I remembered," she replied. Then she looked back down at her book.

"Right," said Sophie, sounding rather annoyed. "We'll go and tell Mrs. Hall we've found you, shall we? Because everybody's running around the school worried about you!"

Ellie saw Isabelle's face flash to surprise. Isabelle opened her mouth to say something, but Sophie turned and pulled Ellie away.

"Honestly!" Sophie snorted as they hurried off to find Mrs. Hall. "Who does that girl think she is?"

Dear Diary,
    I am writing in bed. Must be quick as there are only a few minutes before lights—out. It's still freezing outside and the atmosphere here in the dorm is even colder. Isabelle caused the most almighty panic today when we all thought she was missing, lost in the snow, and she doesn't even seem to care that we cared! Sophie has had it with her completely, but something in me just won't let me dismiss Isabelle like that. I still can't help wondering if there is something else that makes Isabelle so hard to get along with.

"Today we're going to begin preparing the routines for your forthcoming ballet appraisals," Ms. Wells told the Year 7 girls at the start of ballet class a few days later. "After warm-up and barre work, the routines move to the center with *port de bras*, followed by *adage* and *pirouettes*. Then pointe work, followed by *petit allégro*, before finishing with *grand allégro*."

Ms. Wells took them through the warm-up stretches and then the routine she'd set at the barre. To Ellie's relief, there was nothing there for her to worry about—a series of *petits battements* and the quick, energetic *battements frappés* that she could perform in her sleep, followed by the slower, more graceful *développés*.

Then they moved into the center of the studio to run through the *port de bras*. Ms. Wells took them through a fairly difficult sequence that involved bending the body forward, sideways, and backward, while they moved their arms through a series of positions.

Still, Ellie thought, after they'd practiced the *port de bras* a few times through, it was nothing she hadn't done before. With plenty of practice, she should be fine.

Next were the graceful *attitudes* and *arabesques* of the slow tempo *adage* section, followed by a sequence of *pirouettes* and then *petit batterie* and *grand allégro* jumps. And finally, it was time for the pointe work section, which Ellie was particularly dreading. They hadn't practiced the new step, the *pas de bourrée piqué*, since the first disastrous time Ellie had attempted it, and Ellie certainly wasn't looking forward to a repeat performance of her failure. As the students weren't allowed to practice *en pointe* without supervision until they were older and more experienced, Ellie had replayed the movement again and again in her head, and had practiced as best as she could in soft shoes. But now . . . Now it was time to get it right. And she *would* get it right!

As the class stretched their feet with a series of slow rises and *échappés en pointe*, Ellie caught sight of a frown on their teacher's face.

"Sophie, your instep is falling outwards," Ms. Wells said, bending down to push Sophie's foot into place. "Back down again, everybody," she ordered. She squatted down at Sophie's feet. "Sophie, let me have a closer look," she requested, holding one of Sophie's feet in her hand and frowning slightly at the instep. "You are going to have to do some extra work on these feet of yours, Sophie Crawford," she said. "The physio did give you some exercises to build up your instep, didn't she?"

Sophie nodded, blushing wildly.

Ellie remembered how, in the first week of term, the shoe-fitter who'd come to fit them all for new ballet shoes had also told

Sophie she'd have to do extra work to increase the flexibility of her instep. Lara, too, had been given a set of exercises—but in her case, it was to strengthen her almost-too-flexible "banana feet," with their high instep. Ellie knew that Lara had worked diligently on her problem feet, but Sophie . . . well, Sophie hadn't, really.

Sophie scuffed her toe along the floor awkwardly. "I guess I'll have to work on it a bit harder," she said.

Ms. Wells nodded. "If you're serious about becoming a ballet dancer, Sophie, you should be working on these feet every single night—and every other chance you get," she said solemnly. "Strong, supple feet make all the difference to a dancer's performance." She glanced around the room. "I think we all know, nothing comes easily in this game."

Like we need reminding! Ellie thought, wincing at her tingling toes. Ballet was a far cry from the prancing around in frilly tutus and tights like some people thought it was. She knew it meant years of hard, hard training, of sweating and aching and working your body through the most grueling routines.

Yet it was all worth it, to be able to dance. There was no way Ellie would rather do anything else in the world, however hard she had to work.

"Okay," Ms. Wells said, smiling around the room. "We'll try the *pas de bourrée piqué* again next. We'll run through it a few times at the barre, like last time, and then you can try it in the center." She went through the movement to remind them what she wanted them to do, and then clapped her hands expectantly.

"Your turn now," she said. "Off you go."

Ellie gritted her teeth. *Come on, Ell,* she told herself, trying to feel positive about the new step. *Here we go!*

She tried to remember everything Ms. Wells had told them as she began. *Pick up, step, pick up, close. Weight forward, over the toes. Don't lean back!*

She took a deep breath and picked up her left leg, transferring her weight onto the right toes. No! She'd done it too quickly and knocked herself off balance.

"Take your time, Ellie," Ms. Wells said encouragingly. "There's no rush. Keep trying. I know you can do it."

Ellie tried to smile at her teacher's kind expression, but she couldn't help noticing that everybody else seemed to be managing fine without any such encouragement. There was Grace, her cheeks radiant with happiness as she performed the step effortlessly, and Bryony, concentrating hard. And of course, there was Isabelle, dancing the *pas de bourrée piqué* as if she'd been doing it for as long as she could walk.

I will do this if it kills me, Ellie thought grimly as she prepared to start again. She took another deep breath, remembering her teacher's words. *Take your time, Ellie . . .*

Okay. Left foot up, nice and smoothly, no rush, and . . . onto the right toes! Ellie was expecting to wobble over yet again, but to her great surprise, she stayed still, balancing perfectly on one foot for a moment.

"What did I tell you?" Ms. Wells said, smiling. "Lovely! Keep that weight forward. Yes, you've got it!"

Ellie beamed, keeping her weight on one foot for far longer than necessary, simply because it felt so darn good to have achieved the balance. She'd done it! She'd actually done it!

"Don't forget to finish off the movement," Ms. Wells joked. "Step to the side and pick up the other foot."

Ellie carefully did so, trying not to clutch at the barre. And up she went onto her left foot. Sweat broke out on her forehead and her foot throbbed with the sheer exertion of holding up her entire body weight, but she felt absolutely wonderful.

Lara gave her the thumbs-up from across the room, and Grace grinned broadly at her. In some ways, Ellie reflected, coming down onto the floor again, it was even *better* to struggle with a step and then experience the glory of conquering it, rather than be able to do everything straightaway.

"Now let's try the same thing in the center," Ms. Wells said, returning to the front of the studio. "It's exactly the same step, but this time you don't have the barre to help you."

Ellie's mouth felt dry as she moved reluctantly away from the barre and into the middle row of girls in the center of the studio. She had only just gotten it at the barre.

The pianist began to play, and Ms. Wells counted them in. "And . . . pick up! Step! Pick up! Close! Pick up! Step! Pick up! Close!"

The tempo seemed faster than at the barre. It was *too* fast, Ellie thought, close to tears as she wobbled off balance again and again. She simply couldn't keep up.

"Go back to the barre to practice if you're finding it a struggle," Ms. Wells said calmly, over the music. "There is plenty of time to get this right."

Ellie slunk back to the barre, her cheeks hot. It was all she could do not to cry. Just for a few minutes, she'd felt as if she'd conquered the difficult step. Yet now, it felt as if she was straight back to square one.

Dear Diary,

I'm so disappointed in myself. Why am I struggling so much with the pas de bourrée piqué? I thought I had it for a moment, but when I moved from the barre to the center, I lost it again. I've just got to get this right. I've got to!

The other girls have been great about it—really supportive. They know it's bugging me and they keep telling me that lots of ballerinas have their weak spot. Lara says she finds the port de bras hard, and Grace still isn't confident about the temps levé. But the pas de bourrée piqué is all I can think about now. Why can't I do it? Why can't I do it?!

I've never really had to struggle with any step like this before. I hate feeling like my

body won't do what I want it to. I just
know I'm going to dream about it tonight!

Sophie's just caught sight of my miserable
face and says she's going to do my horoscope
to cheer me up. Let's hope she predicts some
success for me soon!!

On the following Saturday afternoon, Grace, Lara, Sophie, and
Bryony were planning to join a school shopping trip into Sheen,
the nearby neighborhood. For once, Ellie didn't feel like joining
them.

Though Ms. Wells had told them they weren't allowed to
practice in their pointe shoes unsupervised yet, Ellie still felt the
urge to do *something*. Maybe a hard bout of jumping would clear
the niggling doubts that had been in her head all week. Since her
struggle with the *pas de bourrée piqué*, Ellie's usual confident *I
can do it, I can do it* motto had been replaced by *I can't do it! I
can't do it! What if I can't ever do it?*

In the studio, she warmed up and started practicing her *temps
levé*. What was it Ms. Wells had said to her the other day? She
needed to be more vertical. She watched herself critically in the
wall mirrors. Yes, she could see what Ms. Wells meant: She was
pulling her upper body back. Maybe if she . . .

Just then, the door swung open, and Isabelle walked in.

Both girls looked at each other in surprise.

"Pardon," Isabelle said in French. "Sorry, I mean," she added.

"I did not know anyone would be in here. I can go next door—"

"That's okay," Ellie replied easily. "There's room for two. I was just trying to get my *temps levé* right."

Isabelle pulled off her new sneakers and pristine sweatpants and put on her ballet shoes. "Yes, I saw you had a problem with those," she said.

Ellie bristled at Isabelle's frankness. *We can't all be perfect!* she felt like snapping.

Isabelle began warming up at the far end of the studio, and Ellie went back to work. She had been practicing her *temps levé* across the studio, as they'd done with Ms. Wells earlier in the week, but now decided to do a few *sur place,* or on the spot. Now that Isabelle was here, Ellie felt slightly self-conscious about soaring across the studio, and, no doubt, getting it all wrong in front of her.

Ellie stood in fifth position, ready to begin, she then stepped forward into the jump, throwing her leg up in *arabesque* behind her. She frowned at her reflection. Still not quite there. What was the secret to getting it right?

As she landed, sighing to herself, she saw in the mirror that Isabelle was approaching her.

"You're doing it wrong. Watch me; I'll show you," Isabelle said.

Though it had come out a little rude, Ellie realized with surprise that Isabelle was offering to help. She nodded.

The French girl performed the movement flawlessly.

Ellie groaned, "How do you do it? I just don't know what I'm doing wrong."

"I think you are too tense. You need to relax!" Isabelle said. "Go toward your front arm. The way I learned this jump, we concentrate on the line first, *then* you can build up the height."

Ellie felt a little downcast at the advice. Going high was the best thing about the *grand allégro* jumps, in her opinion! "It's worth a try," she said. "Thanks."

Isabelle watched critically as Ellie tried again. Ellie was watching herself, too. Up she went, pushing off the ground, before landing.

"Don't look in the mirror," Isabelle advised. "Now you are distracting yourself. Try again with your eyes shut. Just tell yourself to be a straight line in the air. Don't think about how high you are going. Jumping lower but being straight is better than being out of line."

Ellie couldn't help a small smile at the French girl's earnest expression. For once, she didn't mind that Isabelle seemed to know everything. It was actually pretty helpful. Isabelle clearly had a talent and a passion for ballet. And she seemed to really *want* to help Ellie get the movement right. Maybe there *was* a nice side to Isabelle Armand, after all.

Then, feeling slightly self-conscious, Ellie obediently shut her eyes. "You're the boss," she joked. "Okay, here I go."

Up she went again, throwing her leg out as cleanly and strongly as possible, all the while reminding herself to be a vertical line, head lifted slightly . . .

And she was down again, opening her eyes to see a broad smile on Isabelle's face! "You did it, Ellie!" she cried. "That was *très bien*! Ms. Wells could not do it better, I think!"

Ellie laughed, a little surprised to see Isabelle smiling happily for the first time. "Thank you," she said warmly. "Thanks so much! You should hire yourself out as a personal tutor, Isabelle!"

Isabelle smiled and spread her hands out expressively. "Ahh, Ellie, but I don't think the students would be queuing up for ME, *non*?"

Ellie thought about the times when Isabelle's sharp tongue had offended her friends. Would they ever be able to forgive and forget? "Well, maybe," Ellie joked, wagging a finger. "Once I've spread the word that Isabelle Armand gives private coaching, you'll . . ."

RING! RING!

Both girls jumped.

"Is that your phone?" Ellie asked.

Isabelle looked startled, as if she'd never heard it ring before. "I think it must be," she said, going to the corner of the studio and rummaging around in her bag. "Sorry, Ellie."

"It's all right," Ellie said, getting in position to practice another jump. She was feeling rather stunned at the last few things they'd said to each other. Who would have thought that she, Ellie Brown, would be sharing a joke with Isabelle? Why, for a minute, it was almost as if they were *friends*!

She glanced over at Isabelle, who had pulled out a small silver cell phone. As soon as Isabelle saw the caller display, her face lit up. *"Maman!"* she cried happily into the phone. "Hello! How are you? I was wondering—" She broke off to listen, but as she did so, her face darkened.

Ellie looked away quickly, not wanting to be nosy. It was Isabelle's mom, that much was clear. But from the furious-sounding torrent of French that Isabelle was now rattling off, the call wasn't going too well.

Ellie felt rather uncomfortable as she did a few more jumps against the backdrop of Isabelle's fury. Then she decided to go. Enough was enough, and perhaps she should leave Isabelle to her privacy. Isabelle was still shouting angrily into the phone, her dark eyes stormy.

Just as Ellie was slipping off her ballet shoes, on the verge of creeping out, Isabelle jabbed a button on her cell phone peevishly. "I cannot believe it!" she cried in English.

Ellie froze. "Um . . . are you okay?" she asked tentatively.

"Idiote!" Isabelle stormed, glaring at the phone. "Oh—sorry, I don't mean you, Ellie. My mother. I do not understand that woman!"

Ellie felt very awkward. She wished somebody else were here with her, somebody who would know the right thing to say. Calm Bryony, or sensitive Grace would know just how to comfort Isabelle. "Was it . . . was the phone call bad news?" Ellie asked hesitantly.

Isabelle sighed heavily. "My *mother* is bad news," she raged. The phone began ringing again in her hand. Isabelle took one look at it and hurled it at the wall in the corner of the studio. The phone cracked open and stopped abruptly, mid-trill.

Ellie hesitated awkwardly. "Um . . ." she mumbled, not sure what to say.

Isabelle stuck her chin in the air. "I am going to do some big, big jumps, I think," she announced. "I will *dance* her out of my head!"

Without another word, Isabelle launched into a perfect set of *temps levé*s, far higher than Ellie had ever jumped, with a savage set to her face.

Ellie hovered by the door. "Well . . . If you want to talk about it, come and find me," she called, and then, when Isabelle made no reply, Ellie left her, with something approaching relief as she made her escape. Phew! More fireworks from the new girl! Whatever could Isabelle's mom have done to upset her so?

Dear Diary,

What a strange day. Although it sounds like the others had a great time in Sheen this afternoon (I've got a mouth full of candy from Lara to prove it!), I'm glad I stayed here. I've got my temps levé straightened out—AND I got to know Isabelle a little better, though her phone call kind of

brought things in that direction to a halt.
Isabelle just freaked at whatever her mom
said to her. She was soooo furious, it was
actually kind of scary. I just didn't know
what to do. I think she's avoiding me tonight.
She was playing the piano in the Slip earlier
with this don't-speak-to-me look on her
face. You know what? I feel sorry for her.
It must be difficult falling out with your
own mom so far from home.

I told the others that Isabelle had really
helped me with my temps levé, and nobody
could believe it. Sophie joked that I must
have been really terrible to have put Isabelle
in such a mood. I didn't tell them about her
smashing up her phone. It would be kind of
mean to tell them something so personal about
Isabelle behind her back.

I'm actually hoping that, after Isabelle
and I got along okay today in the studio,
we might get to know each other a little
better. For a few minutes there, when we
were having a fun time together, I caught a
glimpse of what a nice person she could be,
once she stopped being so rude! Maybe . . .
just maybe . . . if Isabelle can be nice to me,

she can be nice to everyone?

Oh yeah! Lara said that when they were in Sheen, they were following some of the Year 7 boys and snooping at what they bought. Oliver Stafford spent a ton on a bottle of cologne, they said! That boy is soooo vain!

Better go—Sophie's promised to do my hair with her new straightening irons!

Chapter 7

In their very next ballet class, after barre and center work, Ms. Wells asked the girls to line up at one side of the studio. "Let's practice some *temps levés*," she said.

Ellie looked over at Isabelle and smiled. Even though the girls hadn't spoken since their practice session in the studio, Isabelle gave a little smile back.

When it was Ellie's turn to jump across the studio, she took a deep breath and tried to remember everything that Isabelle had said. *I am a straight line; I am a straight line,* she told herself as she took off. Previously she'd concentrated hardest on the height of her jumps. Now she made sure she had every movement precise and correct. She wouldn't even *think* about how high she was going, she vowed.

"Very nice, Ellie!" Ms. Wells said warmly. "Much better! Perfect positioning in the air—lovely and straight!"

Ellie glowed with the praise and mouthed "thank you" to Isabelle. Isabelle, in turn, did a little curtsey back to her and smiled.

The rest of the class passed in a happy blur. After the lesson,

Sophie came over to congratulate Ellie on her jumping. "I didn't think Isabelle would be nice enough to help *anybody,* but after seeing you jump like that, I actually believe she did help you!" she said.

Unfortunately, Isabelle, who was pulling on her red sweatpants a few feet away, had heard every word. "I am right here, you know," she said stiffly. "Maybe you should stick to talking about me behind my back, like you usually do."

Sophie spun around, looking guilty. "Sorry," she said, holding her palms up. "No offense. I . . . uh . . . meant it as a compliment." Then she smiled. "Hey, do you think if you helped *me,* I'd be jumping like that, too?"

Isabelle sniffed. "I doubt it, Sophie," she said. "I could help Ellie because she is a good dancer. But you—you dance like a carthorse!"

"Hey!" spluttered Sophie, stung by the harsh words. "No, I do not!"

"I hardly think they'd let a 'carthorse' into The Royal Ballet School, Isabelle," Lara said dryly. "Sophie is a great dancer, like all of us are."

Isabelle snorted. "Sure," she said, her voice dripping with sarcasm.

"Isabelle—" Ellie began reproachfully, but Isabelle was already striding out of the studio. She felt bad for Isabelle that she'd heard Sophie saying unkind things about her, but even so, she didn't have to call Sophie names in return. Why couldn't she be as Ellie had seen her before, friendly and . . . well, nice?

"Stuck-up *Mademoiselle*! I wish she'd never come here!" Sophie muttered, her face still flushed with embarrassment.

Dear Diary,
    Just as I think I'm starting to understand Isabelle, she turns even ruder than ever! After today's outburst to Sophie, I wonder whether I've imagined laughing with Isabelle in the studio on Saturday. How can anyone be so nice one minute and so horrible the next?

·   ·   ·   ·

It was the weekly choreography class at the end of the following day. Ms. Denton announced that she wanted the girls to work on short routines to a piece of music from *Sleeping Beauty*.

"Split up into groups of four," she told them, "and imagine it's the first time you've ever heard the music. As you listen, try to work out what it means to you. How does it make you feel? How does it make you want to dance?"

Sophie joined Ellie and Grace, while Lara and Bryony went over to form a group with Megan and Holly. Kate, Alice, Scarlett, and Rebecca were the third group. Only Isabelle was left alone.

"Isabelle, join Grace's group," Ms. Denton told her.

Grace sighed. "I hope she isn't going to be a diva about this," she muttered to Ellie so Ms. Denton couldn't hear.

Isabelle glared at Grace, who turned crimson. It was obvious that she had heard. "So, if I am to be a diva, what will that make *you*, then, Grace? A doormat?" Isabelle retorted under her breath.

Before Grace could reply, Ms. Denton began to speak again. "Listen to the music, first of all," she said. "Close your eyes and think about the atmosphere it conjures up. Ready? Here it comes."

Ellie was relieved to shut her eyes and listen to the calming notes of *Sleeping Beauty*, yet she could barely concentrate on the music. The only atmosphere she was picking up on was the *bad* atmosphere in the group!

Ellie was dreading the music ending, and any more bickering to break out between Grace and Isabelle. Yet when Grace made the first tentative suggestions about how they should choreograph the piece, instead of continuing the argument, Isabelle merely nodded demurely and went along with Grace's directions.

Ellie tried hard not to show her surprise as Isabelle allowed Grace to position her for the opening steps without another murmur. Grace asked her three dancers to stand in a straight line, but Sophie was frowning.

"Grace, do you think maybe if I am in the middle, not Isabelle, that would work better?" Sophie asked.

Grace hesitated. "Well, I put Isabelle in the middle and you at the back, because you're taller than Isabelle," she pointed out. "And Ellie goes at the front because she's the smallest."

"But if I go in front of Isabelle, then . . ." Sophie started.

Isabelle was shaking her head. "Grace is the choreographer," she said firmly. "And I think she is right. We will stay where she has put us, I think."

The four of them carried on with the piece and Isabelle worked hard throughout, taking direction without arguing about it each time. Sophie, however, was an aspiring choreographer, too, and had her own ideas about how the routine should be danced. Every time Sophie questioned one of Grace's decisions, Ellie noticed that Isabelle would back up Grace. It was almost as if she felt bad about her "doormat" remark and was trying to make it up to her somehow, Ellie thought. Whatever the reason, it was a pleasant surprise to be dancing with Isabelle in this kind of mood. When she wasn't being contrary and rude, she did seem to be a different person.

When the lesson was almost over, Ms. Denton asked each group to perform their routine. Ellie, Isabelle, and Sophie danced well, and even earned their choreographer, Grace, a word of praise from Ms. Denton.

"Very nice," she said, nodding her head approvingly. "Good teamwork—and lovely choreography, Grace. Well done!"

Ellie elbowed Grace proudly, who was flushed pink with pleasure.

"Thanks, guys," Grace said as they left the studio. "Thanks, Soph, thanks, Ellie. And thanks, Is—"

But Isabelle was already striding ahead without hearing. It

was as if once the music stopped, so did her friendliness.

•　　•　　•　　•

After choreo, the girls changed and then went down to the canteen for supper. Ellie was tired and aching, and looking forward to refueling her body.

The mail had been delayed that day and was now waiting for them in its usual bundles in the canteen. Ellie rushed over with the others to see if she had received anything and grinned in delight as she spotted a letter with a Chicago postmark on it, addressed in her grandfather's handwriting. She picked it up and then moved from the table to make room for Isabelle, who searched through the envelopes twice over, and then sighed heavily.

Like Ellie, Grace had noticed this. "Are you expecting something important, Isabelle?" she asked tentatively. Ellie guessed she was keen to make up for offending Isabelle earlier. It was just in Grace's nature to feel bad about making the diva comment, even it if was justified!

Isabelle's dark eyes were guarded as they fixed themselves upon Grace. "None of your business," she snapped.

Ellie could see that sensitive Grace was now close to tears. "Come on, Grace," she said, putting her letter into her bag and going over to her friend. "Let's go eat."

As they picked up trays and went to get food, Grace's mouth twisted unhappily. "Why did she have to bite my head off like that?" she asked Ellie. "After she was so . . . normal . . . in choreo just now, too! You know, I was actually starting to warm to her, but now . . . How can somebody be nice one minute and so horrible the next? She's spoiling things for everybody!"

Ellie put her arm around Grace. "Just ignore her," she said. "Forget about it." For all her calming words, inside, Ellie was raging. She hated to see Grace upset. Every time someone tried to reach out to Isabelle, she just got meaner! Even if Isabelle was upset, there was no need to take it out on Grace.

•   •   •   •

Ellie wanted to send some e-mails to her friends in Oxford and Chicago after supper. On her way to the computer room, she passed one of the practice studios, and peeped inside. Isabelle was whirling across the floor, her mouth set in a line, her eyes half-closed in deep concentration.

Ellie wasn't able to resist watching for a few minutes. Despite feeling angry with Isabelle for upsetting Grace, nothing could take away the fact that Isabelle was so good. Ellie watched in admiration as Isabelle spun and leaped. Every student at The Royal Ballet School wanted to be the best dancer they could be, but Isabelle seemed almost obsessed.

Ellie watched her go over to the barre to stretch out her hamstrings, sweating and wild-eyed with the exertion. Before Ellie could slip away, unnoticed, Isabelle looked up and caught her staring in. She stared back questioningly.

Ellie felt awkward. But then she decided that *somebody* had to say something to Isabelle. She couldn't keep treading on people's toes. Besides, Ellie knew Isabelle could be nice when she wanted to be. Sometimes, anyway!

Ellie pushed the door open and strode in. "You know, you really upset Grace earlier," she said. "There was no need to bite her head off. She was only asking you a question."

Isabelle kicked a leg out ferociously, holding on to the barre. "Grace was rude about *me* in choreo," she replied, her dark eyes sparkling with emotion. "She didn't want me in the group, it was obvious. She called me a diva! Then suddenly she's asking personal questions about my life. Why? So she can gossip about me? Or whisper about me like all the other girls?" She glared at Ellie.

Ellie couldn't help it. "If you weren't so rude all the time, nobody would dream of gossiping and whispering about you!" she blurted out.

Isabelle looked shocked, and Ellie tried to soften her next words. "Look, Grace isn't like that. She isn't a gossip. She was just being friendly."

"I don't need any friends," Isabelle said tightly. "I just want to dance."

Ellie shook her head. "Everybody needs friends, Isabelle."

For a moment, Isabelle hesitated, but then she kicked her leg even higher. "Not me," she said. "I don't need anybody." Then she turned her back on Ellie, to kick out her other leg.

Ellie gritted her teeth. Then she shrugged and left the room. "Well, at this rate, you won't *have* anybody," she said quietly.

Dear Diary,

Another day, another drama. Tonight things have calmed down a little, thank goodness. Isabelle hasn't said anything mean; she's mostly avoided us. Grace, Lara, and I have been hanging out in the Slip all evening. Lara played us some tunes on the piano and we had a sing-along. Once they'd gotten over laughing at my singing voice, we had fun. Grace cheered up a little, too. Isabelle really did upset her.

But I know I'd rather hang out with a so-called doormat, who is kind and thoughtful and a true friend, than a pain-in-the-butt diva any day!

Chapter 8

The next couple of weeks seemed to fly by. Ellie's friends could talk of nothing but the appraisals. Sophie even fished out the flexiband the physio had given her back in September and started exercising her feet. Slowly but surely, Ellie had built up her confidence with *pas de bourrée piqué* in the center, to the point where she could *nearly* always do the step without wobbling over. She still dreaded it every time, though. She hated feeling as if she wasn't completely in control of her own feet.

But Grace was still the most anxious whenever the subject of appraisals came up, wondering aloud what the panel of assessors would think of her. Ellie got the feeling that her friend wasn't sleeping well, either; she'd been woken several times by Grace thrashing around in bed or moaning in her sleep.

The only person who never joined in these conversations was Isabelle. Instead of openly stressing about the appraisals like the others, she seemed more withdrawn than ever. She wasn't exactly rude to everybody anymore, but neither was she particularly friendly. She kept her head down and got on with her work alone—that was how she seemed to like it.

Ellie couldn't help feeling a little sorry for Isabelle, even though she knew very well that the new girl had brought this isolation upon herself. Nobody wanted to sit next to her in class, or partner with her in dance lessons or gymnastics. Nobody asked her for help with their French homework, or included her in general conversations. Ellie kept spotting the French girl alone, while the rest of the dorm chuckled over something together. The Royal Ballet School was such a fun, friendly place to be. Isabelle was really missing out! If only she would make the effort to join in, she'd get so much more out of her time at school.

•   •   •   •

A few weeks before the appraisals, Grace was particularly down.

As she and Ellie walked over to the science laboratory together for physics class, Grace confided to her, "Every time I speak to my mum on the phone, she says she's hoping I'll come top in the appraisals. She says it like she's half-joking, but I know she means it. And I just *know* Isabelle will beat me. She's bound to get top spot, isn't she?"

Ellie was surprised. She knew Grace felt pressure, but she had no idea it was so much. "The appraisals aren't a competition," she reminded Grace.

"But we'll still be evaluated," Grace said. "And my mum really wants me to be at the top of the class."

"Come on, Grace," Ellie urged as they entered the science lab. "You're a fantastic dancer! Even if you're not the top of the class, it's not the end of the world."

Grace looked her in the eye. "You reckon?" was all she said.

It was only as Ellie sat down that she realized she'd forgotten to bring her physics homework with her. She must have been so preoccupied that she'd left it on her bed.

She glanced around. Mr. Lewis, their physics teacher, hadn't arrived in the classroom yet. He was almost always a few minutes late. "Back in five! I forgot my homework!" she said to Grace. Then she dashed out of the room and back toward the dorm.

As Ellie raced down the corridor toward the Slip, the telephone on the wall started ringing. She hesitated, uncertain of what to do. She didn't have much time to spare as it was, but she couldn't ignore the trilling phone. It could be something really important.

She snatched up the receiver. "Hello?" she said.

"Hello," came a low female voice in a strange British-French accent. "This is Elise Armand. I am calling to speak to my daughter, Isabelle, if she is around, please."

Ellie's eyebrows shot up in surprise. "Um . . . Isabelle's in a physics lesson at the moment," she replied politely. "May I take a message for her?"

"Yes, please," Isabelle's mom said. "Would you tell her for me that I've been trying to call her on her mobile phone, but I can't get through?"

"I think it's broken actually," Ellie said tactfully, remembering the way Isabelle's cell phone had cracked open on the studio floor.

"That explains it," Mrs. Armand went on. "I've been trying to get hold of her for days and days, to apologize for missing her birthday. I thought she might have lost her phone."

"Oh!" Ellie couldn't help exclaiming. "We didn't know it was Isabelle's birthday. When was it?"

"The eighteenth," Mrs. Armand told her. There was a slight pause. "Anyway, if you could just let her know that, please, I'd be very grateful. And please do tell her that I put a package in the mail for her."

"Sure," Ellie said. "I'll tell her, Mrs. Armand. Good-bye."

Ellie replaced the receiver feeling shocked. It was the beginning of February now—the 18th of January was two weeks ago! Ellie realized that the furious phone conversation she'd witnessed between Isabelle and her mom had taken place around that time.

Imagine forgetting your own daughter's birthday! she thought. No wonder Isabelle had been twitchy about not receiving any mail. How horrible for her, not to have had a single soul wish her a happy birthday.

Ellie hurried to the dorm to pick up her homework and rushed back into the physics lesson. As she sat down beside Grace again, her eyes flicked over to Isabelle who, as usual, was sitting alone at the front of the class. If she *had* announced that it was her birthday, would anybody have made a fuss over her?

Ellie gazed down blankly at her textbook. Ellie could see why Isabelle had kept the whole thing quiet: She had saved herself from being hurt again. It was hardly surprising when her mom had already made it obvious she wasn't *her* top priority.

• • • •

The mail was late again because of the bad weather. It was brought to the canteen and sorted into a bundle for each year as Ellie and the others were finishing their lunch.

Lara went up to claim the bundle for the Year 7 girls and flipped through it eagerly. "Oh!" she exclaimed. "Something for Isabelle today!"

Ellie looked over in interest.

"Two things, actually," Lara went on, still flicking through the pile. "A postcard and a parcel."

Grace raised her eyebrows. "At last," she said. "I think Isabelle had just about given up on receiving anything here."

The girls went up to their dorm and Lara handed out the mail to everybody. Isabelle looked surprised when Lara briskly handed her the postcard and parcel.

Isabelle snatched up her postcard, read it through once, and then flung it onto her bed contemptuously. She didn't even open the parcel. She stuffed it angrily into the bottom of her wardrobe without a second glance. Then she stalked off to English ten minutes early.

Sophie cocked her head. "I wonder what it said," she mused aloud.

"Well," Lara said, "not that I was being nosy, but when I was handing out the mail, I couldn't help but notice that it was posted from New York. And it was all in French."

"Oh!" said Sophie, a little disappointed. "How cosmopolitan!

Makes this letter from my mate Lily, written in English, posted in Manchester, seem *très* dull."

Ellie could guess what it was about, though. She got to her feet. "Think I'll just get some fresh air before English," she told the others, and slipped out of the dorm.

It was kind of true: With the heating on full blast, the dorm had felt a little stuffy, and Ellie wanted to breathe in a few lungfuls of cold, fresh winter air before their next lesson began. But she was also hoping to catch Isabelle on her own, to pass on her mom's message. She knew Isabelle wouldn't thank her for doing that publicly.

As luck would have it, Isabelle was alone in the English room when Ellie walked in a few minutes later.

Ellie came straight to the point. "Isabelle, I wanted to speak to you," she began. "There was a call for you from your mom this morning."

There was a pause.

"Really," Isabelle replied, sounding disinterested. "She has been calling me a lot. Mrs. Hall told me. But I don't want to speak to her."

"She asked me to pass on a message," Ellie went on. "That she's sorry she forgot your birthday and she's sent a parcel." She paused. "I guess that's what arrived today, right?"

Isabelle shrugged. "I don't really care," she said.

Ellie sat down at her usual desk, and took a deep breath. *Here goes nothing*, she thought. "Isabelle, it's awful that your mom forgot your birthday. I'm sorry," she said.

Ellie was braced for the usual, rude "mind-your-own-business" answer. But to her great surprise, Isabelle merely sighed. Then she gave Ellie a half-smile, but her eyes looked sad. "My father forgot, too. That was the postcard. You must be thinking I can't get on with anybody, *non*? Not even my own parents!"

"Well . . ." Ellie began protesting, but then she shrugged. She'd always been a terrible liar. "I don't know," she said feebly.

Isabelle raked a hand through her hair and sighed again. She was silent for a while, thinking. Then she said, "I don't really want to be here, that's all."

"I'd kind of guessed that," Ellie replied wryly.

"My mother said she thinks this is the best place for me because she's moving back to England soon," Isabelle went on. "And she keeps *saying* that, but she's still in France, so who knows?" She paused again, her dark eyes on Ellie as if she was weighing up how much to tell her. "My parents, they just fight, fight, fight," she added. "And neither of them seem to care about me anymore, they're so busy arguing."

Ellie bit her lip. "Sorry to hear that," she said, feeling uneasy under Isabelle's steady gaze.

Isabelle shrugged. "Me too. I can't understand how they have gone from loving each other to hating each other, just like that." She clicked her fingers. "But now my *papa* is in America, and *Maman,* she is all over the place. Both of them are too busy to have me stay over half-term." She sighed again, and stared out the window. "Too busy to remember my birthday, too."

"That must be hard," Ellie said tentatively. *It must be horrendous,* she was thinking inside. *Lonely and miserable and . . .*

Isabelle nodded. "It's like . . . I don't fit in anywhere. Not in America, not in France now either, nor in this country. And definitely not in this school," she said.

"But, Isabelle, if you'd just given people a chance, you might have made some good friends here," Ellie said, then added quickly, "You still could."

Isabelle looked resolute. "What would be the point?" she asked. "My mother may change her mind next month, and I'll be back in Paris. Or we'll be somewhere else. Australia, knowing her. Or Japan. Or . . ."

". . . Or you might be here for the next four years. In which case, you *had* better start making some friends! And besides, I've moved around a lot in the past year and I've kept my friends, even though I'm far away." Ellie leaned forward. "Isabelle, most people here are awesome. You'd have a lot more fun if you got to know them. They could . . . help you."

Isabelle bristled at the word "help." It was the wrong thing to say to somebody so proud, Ellie realized, a moment too late.

They both turned their heads at the sound of footsteps approaching the classroom, and heard Sophie laughing about something or other. But Sophie stopped abruptly when she saw Isabelle.

"Hmph," Isabelle said stiffly. She didn't look convinced.

Dear Diary,

I found out a whole lot more stuff about Isabelle today. I'm starting to see why she's been so offhand with everybody. I guess if you thought you might be uprooted at any moment to another life in yet another country, you might make less of an effort to fit in someplace. And I guess if your parents aren't getting along, it would make you feel angry with the whole world, like everything's out of control and you can't trust anybody anymore.

I do feel sorry for her. Imagine her parents forgetting her birthday AND being too busy for her in half-term! I'd be so miserable and hurt; I know it would make ME bad-tempered and moody. No wonder she throws everything into her dancing. It's all she's got.

What can I do, though? Now that Isabelle's been so rude to everyone here, it's hard to imagine them ever getting along. If only she would make the effort . . .

"Come on, let's have a game of something," Ellie ordered her friends. She stood right in front of the common room TV screen to get their attention, and put her hands on her hips. "It's Sunday afternoon, remember? The weekend! You know, like when you have time off to do fun stuff together? Everyone looks like their dog just died or something."

Grace pulled a face from where she was sitting on one of the squashy sofas. "Yeah, because the appraisals are next week!" she replied.

"I know that, but worrying about it isn't doing anybody any good," Ellie said firmly. She turned around and switched off the soap opera that some of the girls had been watching. "And *that* isn't helping, either," she said firmly. "Too depressing."

"Hey! I need to know if Grandma Bell is going to survive her operation!" Sophie protested, making a lunge for the remote.

"I already checked in the TV guide, and we won't know until Tuesday," Ellie told her, hiding the remote behind her back. "Come on, guys. Look at us all, moping around. Let's play Truth or Dare; that'll cheer everybody up!"

There were a few grumbles, but Bryony put down her magazine and Grace stopped writing her letter.

"You too, Isabelle," Ellie ordered, much to the surprise of the rest of the girls. "Put down that book at once!" Her heartbeat quickened, expecting Isabelle to refuse to join in. She could see Sophie looking at her strangely, wondering why she was encouraging Isabelle to join the rest of them.

Isabelle was looking just as surprised to be asked.

"Come on," Ellie said for a third time. "Let's *all* play. Isabelle, it would be kind of nice for us all to do something together before the appraisals start and we get even more stressed out." Ellie stopped, then said pointedly, "You know, it might help . . ."

"Some of us couldn't *get* any more stressed out," Grace muttered, but, like the rest of the girls, she watched in surprise as Isabelle obediently closed her book.

"Okay, I'll play," Isabelle said. "What is this game, Truth or Dare?"

"Oh, it's really easy," Ellie went on briskly, trying to hide how pleased she was that Isabelle had agreed to join in. Ever since the pair of them had talked about Isabelle's family in the English room the week before, she'd been looking for ways to get Isabelle more involved in school life. When Grace had missed classes on Tuesday with a bad cold, Ellie had sat next to Isabelle instead, claiming she wanted company. She felt that Isabelle was gradually thawing with her, getting to trust her a little more, but she still wasn't part of the group as far as the other girls were concerned. Isabelle was going to *have* to make the effort, and Ellie was determined to give her the opportunity.

Ellie was hoping that a game of Truth or Dare could make even the most private person at The Royal Ballet School open up a teeny bit. "All you do," she explained to Isabelle, "is choose either to tell the truth to a question the other girls ask you, or do a dare. And if you fail . . ."

"Forfeits," Lara said, with a gleam in her eye. "Something horrible, like empty the laundry bin every day for the last week, or wash Sophie's stinky feet for her!"

Sophie waved her bare feet in the air, and everybody giggled nervously. Her eyes glittered as she looked over at Isabelle. "Isabelle, are you sure you want to play? You might end up with my feet, after all—and we all know how icky a *carthorse's* feet get!"

Ellie held her breath. *Oh, no,* she thought. They were off to a flying start, with Sophie choosing that moment to dredge up the insulting name Isabelle had called her all those weeks ago!

Isabelle flinched. "I should not have said that," she said, meeting Sophie's gaze. "You are not a carthorse. And I am sorry."

Sophie raised her eyebrows. She'd obviously been expecting an argument over it, instead of an apology, Ellie realized.

"Apology accepted," Sophie said, after a moment.

"Right, well, anyway," Ellie said hurriedly, wanting to move on. "Let's think of a forfeit, guys. Something truly horrendous. How about . . . if you fail to answer truthfully or you refuse the dare, you have to . . ." She paused. "You have to . . . um . . ."

"Sneak into the boys' dorm . . ." Lara suggested.

". . . And bring back a souvenir," Bryony spluttered. "Matt's socks!"

"And then you have to send him a ransom note, saying 'If you want these back, you have to buy us all some chocolate,' " Sophie giggled.

Grace was shaking her head. "Too mean," she said. "And far too complicated! We've got to keep it simple."

"What, then?" Sophie asked.

There was a pause while they all thought, then Isabelle's eyes brightened. "Perhaps the forfeit could be that you have to stand up at suppertime and say in a really loud voice that you are in love with Mr. Best," she said mischievously.

Everybody burst into giggles at the thought. Ellie really liked Mr. Best, their funny, friendly math teacher, but she was quite sure that his short, plump figure and balding head did nothing to inspire feelings of love in any of the students!

"Ooh, that's a toughie," Sophie said, giving Isabelle an admiring look. "But I like it! What does everyone else think?"

Grace was shuddering. "It is awful," she declared. "There's no way anybody's going to duck out of a dare now, though!"

"Right, that's settled, then. The Mr. Best announcement is our forfeit," Ellie said, grinning at Isabelle. "And I'll go first," she volunteered. "I'll have . . . Truth." She added in an aside to Isabelle, "Now you guys get to think of a question for me. But be gentle, please!"

"No chance," Lara said cheerfully. "Now, what do we all really want to know about our very own Ellie Brown?"

Kate opened her mouth first. "Ellie, tell the truth, do you fancy Matt?" she asked.

Ellie's eyes widened in shock. "Matt Haslum? No!" she squealed. "He's just a friend!"

"I hope you're telling the truth, Ellie," Sophie said warningly. "There's a bit of a close partnership between you two in character classes, after all. Now, is that your final answer?"

"Yes!" laughed Ellie, trying to sound indignant. "Matt and I are just buddies."

"Do we believe her, or shall we make her do the forfeit?" Lara asked teasingly.

"We believe her," Grace said. "Ellie—you're off the hook!"

"Okay, then I'll have a turn," Lara said. "And I'll have a Dare. Hit me with it, girls!"

"A dare?" Isabelle repeated. "You mean, we have to dare you to do something?"

"Exactly," Bryony said. She hesitated for a moment, then turned to Isabelle. "Got any other good ideas, Isabelle? The more outrageous, the better!"

Isabelle jumped as if she was surprised to have been asked. Then her brow wrinkled as she thought. "Let me see . . ." she pondered.

"How about . . . kissing Oliver Stafford?" Grace giggled.

"Too, *too* mean," Ellie decided with a shudder. "Even

for Lara."

"Okay, sending him a valentine," Sophie suggested. "It's Valentine's Day soon, isn't it? And we dare you to send Oliver a valentine card and sign it from yourself."

"Nooooo!" wailed Lara.

"YESSSS!" the others cheered.

Somebody started a chant up. "Dare! Dare! Dare!"

Lara groaned and shook her head. "I'm not friends with any of you lot now," she said. "But I'll accept the dare."

"She's tough," Sophie marveled as the cheers rose up again. "Attagirl, Lara, we knew you would!" She got up and went over to the arts and crafts cupboard. "And just so you don't accidentally forget . . . you can do it right now," she said, winking at the other girls. "Look, here's a nice bit of red card. Perfect!"

Ellie glanced over at Isabelle to see what she made of this game so far, as Sophie pulled out some pens and glitter. To her joy, the French girl was grinning at Lara's disgusted face along with everybody else.

"All right, all right," Lara sighed. "You win!" She folded the card and drew a rather wonky heart on the front. "What shall I write inside it?"

"I could drown in your blue eyes . . ." Sophie declaimed melodramatically.

Lara frowned. "I thought he had brown eyes?" she asked.

Sophie was grinning. "Exactly—he does." She chuckled. "How insulting, though, to get it deliberately wrong!"

Grace shook her head. "We don't want insults, though, we want messages of undying love," she said. "How about: When Irish eyes are smiling . . ."

"No chance," Lara said firmly. "I'm not putting anything in about being Irish. I don't want him to know it's from me!"

"The dare was to send Oliver a card and sign it, remember," Ellie put in. "No backing out now, McCloud . . . otherwise you'll be declaring your love for Mr. Best instead!"

Lara pulled a face. "Oh, you horrible girls," she groaned. "To think I saw you as my friends!"

"Perhaps you could write something in French," Ellie put in, glancing over at Isabelle, trying to keep her involved. "After all, that's the language of love, isn't it?"

"And Oliver will be too thick to understand it, hopefully," Lara agreed, brightening at the suggestion. "Isabelle, will you help me?"

"Of course," Isabelle said, looking pleased once again to be asked. Then she snorted with amusement as a thought struck her. "I know! You could put: *Oliver, je t'adore, mon petit chou!*"

"What does that mean?" Sophie asked.

"It means, 'Oliver, I love you, my little darling,' " Isabelle said, "but literally translated, it means, 'Oliver, I love you, my little cabbage.' So if he has to look up *'chou'* in the dictionary, he'll think that you're calling him a 'cabbage'!"

The girls all hooted with laughter. "Fantastic!" Sophie spluttered, once she'd gotten her breath back. "Absolutely spot on, Isabelle!"

Lara carefully wrote the words in, glued some glitter around, and then put the card to one side with a shudder. "There," she said. "One valentine card for Mr. Stafford. One dare complete!"

"Who's next?" Bryony asked. Again, she hesitated, then asked, "Isabelle, do you want your go?"

There was a moment's hesitation, and then Isabelle nodded. "I am not going to choose a dare," she said, "because if I had to send Oliver Stafford a valentine card, too, I think I would have to run away from this school in shame."

Lara chuckled. "I don't blame you," she said. "In fact, that's not a bad idea. So . . . it's Truth, then?"

Isabelle nodded again, looking slightly apprehensive. "But you know, if you ask me anything really awful, I am just going to pretend I do not understand the English," she warned, with a nervous smile.

"Like we're going to fall for a lame excuse like that!" Ellie said, smiling at Isabelle to show that she was only joking.

"Hmmm . . . what shall we ask?" Sophie mused aloud.

The room was silent. There were so many questions that everybody was *burning* to ask Isabelle, but nobody felt they knew her well enough to come out with anything too personal.

Grace, however, was clearly still feeling slightly nettled by the rudeness Isabelle had shown to her previously, and she suddenly burst out with, "Why do you hate The Royal Ballet School so much, Isabelle?" Then she added, "And you have to tell the truth."

Ellie held her breath. She was half-expecting Isabelle not to reply to a question as direct as that. She wouldn't have been at all surprised if Isabelle's face had closed up and she'd marched stiffly out of the common room. *Please go along with the game,* she urged her in her head. *Please tell everybody how you're feeling. They WILL understand; I know it!*

Isabelle fiddled with her fingers. "I don't *hate* it here," she replied warily. She shot a sideways glance at Ellie. "I am just . . . not very happy."

Silence descended, and the light-hearted mood vanished. Ellie guessed that most people were feeling slightly awkward right now. If anybody else in the dorm had said they felt unhappy, she knew that the other girls would have been over like a shot, comforting and supporting the girl in question. But after Isabelle had spent most of the term being rude to everybody, it was a different situation altogether.

"Well, I don't mean to be nosy, but . . . why?" Grace asked after a few moments' silence.

"Are you homesick?" Lara asked gently. Lara had been very homesick the previous term but had fooled everybody into thinking she was happy at school.

Isabelle shook her head. "No. It's not really that." Again, there was that pause, and Ellie guessed she was wondering how much to tell them.

"I don't really *have* a home anymore," Isabelle confessed. "My parents are separating. Everything is changing." She twisted a ring around her finger. "I have felt very angry with them. Angry that they are fighting, angry that they sent me here." She took a deep breath and looked around the room at the other girls. "I know I have not been very nice to some of you, but . . ." She looked directly at Grace, and bit her lip. "I just didn't want to be here. What can I say?" She shrugged apologetically. "I'm sorry," she added in a low voice, her eyes still on Grace.

There was absolute silence in the room.

"Don't worry about it," Grace said at once.

"It's cool," Sophie said.

"We understand," Ellie added.

But Isabelle hadn't finished yet. A single tear rolled down her cheek and she dashed it away impatiently. "You see, I thought that, as long as we stayed in Paris, there might be some hope that my family could sort things out," she confessed. "But when *Maman* said we were leaving, I knew there was no chance."

"How horrible," Lara said sympathetically, passing Isabelle a tissue.

"Have you spoken to your mum lately?" Bryony asked. "Maybe if you told her how you feel, she might . . ."

Isabelle tossed her head. "I broke my phone," she said. "I was so angry with her when she forgot my birthday, I smashed it."

"She forgot your *birthday*?" Sophie echoed, aghast. "Your own mum? No way!"

Isabelle nodded. "*She* forgot, my dad forgot . . ." She looked hurt just thinking about it. "And they are both too busy for me to see them at half-term, so . . ." She spread her hands. "That is why I am angry all the time."

"You can borrow my phone if you want to patch things up with them," Bryony offered at once. "Or even if you want to have a go at them for being so slack!" She patted Isabelle's arm. "As long as you promise not to smash that one, too," she joked.

Sophie leaned forward. "So when exactly *was* your birthday, Isabelle?" she asked curiously. "I've been wondering and wondering what star sign you are. I thought you must be a tempestuous Scorpio, but you must be a . . ."

"Capricorn," Isabelle said.

"Of course," Sophie said, as if everything had fallen into place. "A stubborn old goat . . . oh, in the nicest possible way, of course!"

"Have you opened that package from your mom yet?" Ellie asked quickly, not wanting Isabelle to take offense at being called a goat, when things were going so well. "We couldn't help but see you stuffing it into your closet. She might have sent something really, *really* nice to say sorry."

"Go on, open it," Lara said cheekily. "We've all been dying to know what it is."

Isabelle smiled suddenly. "I will open it right now," she announced.

As she left the common room to get her present, the other girls looked at one another.

"I had no idea," Sophie said bluntly. "No wonder she's been so bad-tempered and stroppy."

"You would be, though, wouldn't you?" Bryony said. "If all that was happening in your own life."

"Poor Isabelle!" Grace said, shaking her head at the things they'd just heard. "How horrible for her."

Isabelle returned just then carrying the parcel. She started ripping off the paper at once to reveal several wrapped presents inside. The first present she opened was a new cell phone, and everybody laughed.

"My mother, she is *determined* to speak to me!" Isabelle groaned. "I will try not to break this one—until our next argument, anyway!"

The second present was a large, expensive-looking box of French chocolates. "What a shame that we are not allowed to keep food in the dorm," Isabelle said, mock sorrowfully. "We will just have to eat them all this afternoon, otherwise Mrs. Hall will be *very* cross with me!"

Everybody laughed, and Ellie felt the tight feeling inside her loosen and relax. She'd been right. There was a nice, funny side to Isabelle underneath all the haughtiness. It was all a matter of persuading Isabelle to show that nice side to other people—and now she had!

●   ●   ●   ●

After several more rounds of Truth or Dare—and a whole box of delicious chocolates later—Ellie got to her feet. "I am all truthed out," she said.

"Me too," Sophie said. "I think I've told you lot enough secrets to keep you going for weeks."

"And agreed to do enough awful dares," Lara groaned, clutching her head as if she was in pain.

"Thanks for the chocolates, Isabelle. They were yummy," Ellie added, smiling across at her. "Now I want to get in some practice before tomorrow. Anyone coming?"

Sophie shuffled her feet, and then shook her head. "I'm too tired," she said, before confessing, "I think there's a good film on soon, anyway."

Grace had gotten up, however. "I'll join you in a few minutes, Ellie. I've just got to give my mum a quick call," she said.

As Ellie went off to the practice studio, she felt really pleased that finally—*finally!*—Isabelle had spent an afternoon with her dorm-mates. And they'd all gotten along! She really hoped that Isabelle would start letting her guard down a bit more often now, and relax with the rest of the girls.

Once inside the studio, Ellie warmed up. She wanted to practice the *pas de bourrée piqué,* the one thing that she still didn't feel confident about, but since she couldn't dance *en pointe* unsupervised, she'd just have to practice the step on half-pointe in her soft ballet shoes. At least she could practice getting the positioning of her body correct, with her weight forward, rather than leaning back and tipping herself off balance.

Ellie was just about to start when the door swung open, and in walked Grace—with Isabelle!

Isabelle came over to Ellie while Grace was pulling on her ballet shoes. "Ellie, thank you," she said, with her usual frankness. "Thank you for asking me to play the truth game. Everybody has been so nice to me today."

"Good," Ellie said, smiling back at Isabelle's solemn face. "I told you they were all right, didn't I?"

"You did," Isabelle said. "So if there's anything I can do for you in return . . ."

Ellie grinned. "I was hoping you'd say that," she confessed. "Because I'm still trying to get my positioning right for the *pas de bourrée piqué.*"

Grace appeared next to them with her ballet shoes on, and cleared her throat. "And I know you helped Ellie with her *temps levé,*" she said, with a small smile on her face. "Is there any chance you could help with mine, too?"

Isabelle laughed and spread her hands expansively. "I will help you both!" she cried. "That is what friends do, yes?"

"Right," Ellie agreed. "Absolutely right!"

Dear Diary,
    Isabelle has been a totally different person today. We had such a good time tonight in the studio! We practiced the pas de bourrée piqué together over and over again and practiced it on demi-pointe. I was leaning back, which made me wobble, so Isabelle kept

her hand on my back while I did it, to keep me straighter, and I could really feel the difference. I feel much more confident now. As for Grace—her temps levé looked fantastic by the time we'd finished practicing. She even gave Isabelle a hug, she was so thrilled. Isabelle went all awkward and squirmy, but I think she secretly liked it. Hooray!

The dorm seems a friendlier place now that people are realizing that Isabelle isn't just moody for the sake of it. I'm writing this in bed, pj's on, etc., and Bryony's just asked Isabelle to help her with her French homework. Isabelle's over there now, going through great long lists of verbs with her. Isabelle even looks different—all flushed and smiley! I never thought I'd see the day when Isabelle Armand was smiley! Maybe it's a sugar overload from the chocolates, but I hope she's starting to feel at home here, too.

Better go. I'm going to phone Pheebs and start making plans for half-term with her. Yay! Not long to go . . . only the appraisal to get through first! GULP!

chapter 10

"I feel sick," Grace moaned, clutching her stomach. "I swear I'm going to be sick."

"You won't be sick," Ellie reassured her, looping an arm through her friend's as they walked to the large Pavlova Studio, where their ballet appraisal was due to take place. "You're just hungry because you didn't have any breakfast, Grace."

"Yeah, because I felt too sick!" Grace wailed. "And now I'm going to be too weak to do anything, and will probably collapse with low blood sugar levels and . . ."

Ellie interrupted her hurriedly. "You are going to be absolutely fine, Grace," she said firmly. "Absolutely, totally, one hundred percent *fine*." She caught sight of Sophie's pale face then. "Are you okay, Soph?"

Sophie forced a lame smile. "Kind of," she said. "It's typical, isn't it? Usually, as a Leo, I just love being the center of attention at all times. But today, I don't want to be the center of attention when I'm falling over!"

"Try to think past this morning, to lunch," Bryony suggested. "What's everybody going to have?"

"Chips," Sophie said immediately. "And chocolate pudding and custard! I'll need some serious comfort food by then."

"Oh, please don't talk about food, I can't bear it!" Grace cried.

A silence fell as they reached the door of the Pavlova Studio. Ellie's heart beat faster than ever and her palms felt clammy with sweat. This was where it would happen! This was what they'd been working toward all term! She felt a hand on her arm, and looked around.

"Good luck, Ellie."

She turned to see Isabelle smiling at her. "Thanks. You too!" Ellie replied.

"Good luck, all of us," Sophie said, a grim expression on her face.

"Amen to that," Grace muttered.

In they went. Lynette Shelton, the Royal Ballet School Director, was waiting for them, along with the Assistant Director and the external panel of assessors. The five adults sat behind a long table at one end of the studio.

"Good morning, everyone," Miss Shelton said with an encouraging smile. "I think you will all recognize Mr. Dowling, our Assistant Director. And this is Ms. Blackwood, Mr. Bourne, and Mr. Lowe, our panel of independent assessors." Miss Shelton paused as the assessors nodded briefly to the girls, then went on, "I am sure you have all rehearsed your work, so relax and enjoy the class. We're not planning any surprises for you!"

There was a nervous murmur of laughter, but Ellie didn't join in. She was too busy checking that her ballet shoes were on properly and trying to stay calm. *In less than two hours, this will all be over,* she reminded herself.

"Ms. Wells, would you like to begin the class?" Miss Shelton invited.

Ms. Wells nodded and her dark eyes flickered over the class. "Everybody ready?" she asked. "Then let's begin."

As the familiar warm-up exercises began, Ellie felt absolutely wired. Adrenaline pumped through her body, and her heart pounded painfully. She tried to calm herself down by breathing deeply through each movement. This helped a little, as did focusing hard on her body's every position, concentrating on getting each detail exact and precise. Her legs felt fluid and strong as they stretched into the familiar *pliés* and *tendus*.

Then Ms. Wells asked them to do the *battement fondu* at forty-five degrees, which involved unfolding one leg from a *coup-de-pied* position *en croix* front, side, and back. "Hold the middle of your backs strongly," she reminded them, "and *up* onto *demi-pointe.*"

Ellie tried to remember everything Ms. Wells had told them about *battements fondues*—that it was a melting, flowing movement, with both legs working smoothly together. She tried to make the move look as seamless as possible as she went up onto *demi-pointe.* Then she breathed in deeply as she held the position, trying not to think about the panel of assessors who were scrutinizing them all, just a few feet away.

"Good," Ms. Wells said warmly as the girls completed their *petit allégro*. The class was going well, and time had flown by through barre work, *adage*, and *pirouettes*. "Now for the *temps levé*."

Ellie caught Isabelle's eye, and pulled a face.

The French girl winked and gave her a nod of encouragement. *No problem, Ellie!* she mouthed.

Lara went first. Ellie could see that she had the jitters from the paleness of her face. It made her red hair and freckles stand out in even sharper contrast than usual. Yet for all her nerves, Lara performed well, with equal distance on the two forward runs that made up the movement.

Bryony went next, and she was good, too. Grace also performed the sequence well, and Ellie could see she was pleased by the huge smile of relief on her face.

Then it was Sophie's turn. Sophie began the move, stepping forward on her right leg and swinging her arms upward and outward into the high V-shape. She hopped in that position with her back leg low.

So far so good, thought Ellie. *Go on, Soph! You can do it!*

Ellie watched as Sophie began to repeat the entire sequence on her left foot. Up and out went her arms once more—but then disaster struck as Sophie skidded on her hop and she tumbled down to the floor!

Ellie could hardly bear to look as her friend scrambled to her feet, red-faced and completed the step. Sophie's hands were shaking, and her mouth twisted downward. Poor Sophie! What a time to fall over!

Before she could think about it anymore, it was her own turn. Ellie put her hands on her hips for a moment and drew in a breath, feeling her ribcage rising. *Don't think about Sophie. Don't think about Sophie,* she ordered herself. *Think about everything you've practiced instead: long arms, strong* arabesque, *head slightly raised . . .*

Off Ellie went onto her right foot, pushing strongly into the air, keeping her arms long and graceful, then into the *pas de chat,* crisp and clean as Isabelle had coached her.

Ellie counted the music in her head as she moved her arms in and across her body again. *Don't pull back! Go toward your front arm!* she could hear Isabelle's voice reminding her in her head. And off she went again, this time on the left foot. Before she knew it, she'd finished, and she just *knew* it had gone well!

As Ellie walked across to the barre with Lara and the others, she heard a burst of applause from the other side of the studio. She looked across in surprise to see Isabelle smiling broadly at her and clapping furiously!

Ellie laughed—and so did everybody else. For the first time since they'd entered the Pavlova Studio, the tension dissolved a little.

Isabelle then seemed to remember where she was and glanced across at the assessors, blushing. *"Pardon,"* she said apologetically.

Luckily, the assessors were all smiling at the French girl's enthusiasm. And then it was Isabelle's own turn and she performed a flawless set of *temps levé* herself.

Ellie grinned as the assessors made their notes. Surely nobody could hold a bit of clapping against somebody so talented?

Next came pointe work. As she went with the others to the side of the studio to put on her pointe shoes, Ellie's palms felt clammy. Okay, this was the big one.

Once Ms. Wells had taken them through the slow rises and *échappés* at the barre, she asked them to come into the center of the studio.

Here we go, thought Ellie, trying to keep her breathing even and slow. She glanced down at her feet. *You can do it,* she told them.

As they began the *pas de bourrée piqué,* it was the strangest feeling, but Ellie could almost feel the imprint of Isabelle's hand on the flat of her back still, keeping her forward as she'd done in practice a few days earlier.

"Pick up, and step, pick up, and close," Ms. Wells instructed.

Ellie concentrated so hard, there was nothing else in her mind but sheer determination to stay on her toes. Up she went onto her left toes, still keeping her back straight and her weight over her toes. It was all she could do not to laugh out loud in relief as she stayed perfectly still on her left foot, before stepping to the side, transferring the weight and going up onto the right.

Ellie gave a sharp intake of breath as she raised her left foot so that all her weight was over her right toes, and held her back straight once more. She was doing it! She was absolutely doing it! She was so excited and proud of herself, she wanted to whip her head around to grin at Isabelle, but just managed not to. But she couldn't help letting her smile through for everyone to see. *Focus, Ellie, stay focused,* she told herself. *It's not over just yet!*

Ellie was so cheered by the success of her *temps levé* and her *pas de bourreé piqué* that she felt relaxed and foot sure for the remaining few minutes of the assessment. She'd conquered her stumbling blocks, and everything else seemed a breeze. Oh, how she loved ballet!

"And . . . thank you," Ms. Wells said.

Ellie felt her face light up with relief. The ballet appraisal was over!

·   ·   ·   ·

Ellie was exhausted for the rest of the day. Now that the whole thing was done, she felt a huge, overwhelming wave of relief.

Everyone looked wiped out by it, Ellie thought, looking around the dorm that evening. It had taken its toll on them all, mentally and physically. Grace, however, was looking happier than she had for weeks. After her perfect *temps levé*, she kept thanking Isabelle over and over again.

"Don't thank me! You did all the work," Isabelle protested laughingly, as Grace mentioned it for the tenth time. "You should thank yourself!"

"Thanks, Grace," Grace giggled, and flopped onto her bed.

"Oh, I think I'm losing it. It's the relief of having got through that awful appraisal!"

"We definitely need to do something to celebrate," Sophie announced, with a shudder. "I can't stop thinking about falling over in the middle of the *temps levé* and how wobbly I was on pointe . . . Oh, I was terrible, wasn't I? Did you see the way I was wobbling all over the place?"

"You were fine," Ellie said sleepily, from her own bed. She'd been concentrating so fiercely on her own pointe work, she'd had no idea until afterward that Sophie had had another nightmare, not quite able to manage her *pas de bourrée piqué* either. But then, Sophie did love to exaggerate. Ellie was sure it couldn't have been as bad as she thought. "Quit worrying, Soph. It's over. But you're right, we do need to celebrate."

Isabelle's phone rang at that point, and she slipped out of the dorm to answer it.

"Don't smash that new phone, now!" Bryony called after her, grinning.

Lara sat up suddenly, looking excited. "I know, we could have a late birthday party for Isabelle!" she suggested, once the dorm door had swung closed behind the French girl.

"Good idea," Ellie said warmly. "I think she would really like that."

"We could get her a cake and some party food from the kitchen," Sophie added. "I'm sure Mrs. Hall would let us, if we explain."

"And it *is* the last week before half-term," Grace said. "And we *have* just had our appraisals. If ever we needed cake and party food, it's now!"

     ●   ●   ●   ●

Ellie and Lara went straight to Mrs. Hall and told her the whole story. Their housemother said she'd help in any way she could, especially as it was the first real Year 7 term-time birthday celebration. The girls who'd already had birthdays the term before, Lara and Megan, had spent their birthdays out of school with their families as they'd coincided with Christmas or half-term. "I'm glad you're all getting along well now," she said. "I got the feeling that things were a little . . . chilly between some of the girls and Isabelle for a while."

Ellie and Lara exchanged glances. "Well . . . I guess so," Ellie said, not wanting to lie. "But everything's fine now. I think we're all going to be friends."

"Good," said Mrs. Hall. "So what shall we order? What sort of cake do you think Isabelle would like?"

"Chocolate," Ellie and Lara both said at once, then giggled. "*French* chocolate, if that's possible," Lara added with a grin.

     ●   ●   ●   ●

With the party food ordered, Ellie started to feel really excited about the forthcoming half-term, the weeklong mid-semester break. She couldn't wait to see her friends in Oxford, and spend time with her mom and Steve.

It seemed like most girls in the dorm were doing something

special. Grace and her mom were spending a few days with their cousins on the south coast. Lara's family was going to stay with her grandparents in County Kerry, a gorgeous part of Ireland. Sophie's family was also going away, to Blackpool, a seaside resort in the north of England, where her grandmother lived.

As far as Ellie could see, Isabelle was the only girl who wasn't much looking forward to half-term. Her mom was still going to be too busy to have her stay, so she was spending the week at school, alone.

"It'll be okay," Isabelle said whenever anybody asked her about it. "I will just practice, practice, and practice until you all come back."

Ellie felt sorry for Isabelle. It wasn't going to be much fun for her, spending a whole week on her own at school, with most of the other students having time away with their families.

Then Ellie had an idea and phoned home from the Slip. "Mom, I know this is short notice," she said, when her mom answered, "but I was wondering if I could have a friend to stay over the half-term vacation?"

Ellie explained the whole story to her mom, who was sympathetic.

"Of course she can stay!" she said. "We'll borrow a camp bed from the Mintons and she can bunk in with you. I think that sounds like a very good idea, Ellie."

Ellie rushed back into the dorm, where she knew Isabelle was doing some prep. "Isabelle!" she cried. "I've just asked my mom if you can stay with me for half-term, and she said yes! Would you like to come and have a week in Oxford?"

Isabelle stared at Ellie in surprise. "You did that for me? I can come and stay at your house?" Her hand fluttered to her throat and then she jumped off her bed and ran over to throw her arms around Ellie. "Thank you, Ellie!" she said. "I would love to!"

"That's settled then!" Ellie said warmly, hugging Isabelle back. "It's a trick really," she added jokily. "I just don't want you practicing too hard without me and getting even better than you already are!"

Isabelle squeezed Ellie even tighter. "You are a good friend, Ellie," she said, sounding choked with emotion. "Just for you, I will not practice for a whole week!"

Both girls laughed. Lara stuck her head around the dorm door just then. "Come in the common room, quick," she said, with a meaningful nod at Ellie. "We're all watching . . . um . . . some of the boys out of the window, and they're doing really funny things!"

Isabelle didn't look convinced by Lara's reason for going to the common room, but Ellie pulled her along, knowing that the other girls had been getting Isabelle's surprise party ready in secret. "Come on, let's have a look," she said.

Isabelle pushed open the door of the common room and gasped at the roar of "Surprise!" that went up around the room.

"We thought 'cos you missed out on a Royal Ballet School birthday last month, Isabelle, we'd have a bit of a party for you tonight instead," Lara explained with a grin.

Isabelle gave a shriek of excitement. Her eyes glittered, and Ellie thought she saw tears shining there. "For me? Oh!" she cried. She gazed around at the other girls with party hats on their heads, and the balloons that had been blown up around the room. "I love this place. Did I tell you that I love this place?" she said, wiping her eyes quickly.

"Have a plate," Lara said, pressing one into her hand. "And tuck in!"

Isabelle looked dazed as she helped herself to the peanuts and potato chips, and the trays of yummy-looking sandwiches. "Thank you," she managed to say. "I am so . . . Oh! I am so surprised!" She wagged a finger at them, smiling. "You girls are very sneaky, you know."

"It's true," Ellie laughed, eating a sandwich happily. "But you wouldn't have us any other way, would you?"

"No," Isabelle declared solemnly shaking her head. "No, I would not!"

After a few minutes, Sophie disappeared out of the room and came back in with the enormous chocolate birthday cake Ellie and Lara had ordered, with twelve lit candles. "Ta-da!" she cried. "How do you say it in French? The *pièce de résistance*!"

"Oh!" cried Isabelle again. "I can't believe it!"

The girls sang "Happy Birthday," and Isabelle blew out the candles in one go.

"Make a wish!" Ellie urged her.

Isabelle's eyes shone as she cut carefully into the cake. "I don't need to," she said, smiling around at the other girls. "One of my biggest wishes has already come true. I feel so happy here at The Royal Ballet School!"

"To The Royal Ballet School!" echoed Sophie, raising her paper cup of juice.

"And happiness," Bryony added.

"And friendship!" Ellie said.

As the girls all raised their cups in a toast, Ellie felt the hairs prickle on the back of her neck. *The Royal Ballet School, happiness, and friendship,* she thought again to herself, with a rush of joy. What more could a girl possibly ask for in life?

GLOSSARY

ROYAL BALLET METHOD: An eight-year system of training and methodology developed and utilized by The Royal Ballet School to produce dancers with clean, pure classical technique

ADAGE: From the musical direction *adagio*, meaning slow; slow work with emphasis on sustained positions and on balance

ALLÉGRO, GRAND ALLÉGRO, PETIT ALLÉGRO: Jumps that can be performed at various speeds

ARABESQUE: One leg is extended to the back (the name is taken from the flourished, curved line used in Arabic motifs)

ATTITUDE: *Grande pose*; one leg in the air with the knee bent either to the front or back

BALANCÉ: To rock; a swinging three-step movement transferring weight from one foot to the other

BARRE: The horizontal wooden bar fastened to the walls of the ballet classroom or rehearsal hall that the dancer holds for support

BATTEMENT: To beat; a beating of the legs; see *grand battement, petit battement,* and *battement frappé* for variations

BATTEMENT FONDU: To melt; a movement on one leg, bending and extending both legs at the same time

BATTEMENT FRAPPÉ: To strike; a striking action of the working foot

BRAS BAS: The rounding of the arms held in front of the thighs with a small space between the hands

CHASSÉ also PAS CHASSÉ: A gliding step when the leg slides out and the other leg is drawn along the floor to it

COUP DE PIED: Around the "neck" of the foot; one pointed foot is placed at the calf—just above the ankle—of the opposite leg

CROISÉ: To cross; a diagonal position with one leg crossed in front of the other

DEMI-PLIÉ: A small bend (of the knees) in alignment over the toes, without causing the heel, or heels, of the foot to lift off the floor

DEMI-POINTE: Rising *en pointe* only halfway, onto to the ball of the foot, not completely onto the toes

DEVELOPPÉ: The unfolding of the working leg; the leg is drawn to the knee and then extended from there

ECHAPPÉ: To escape (a movement that begins in 5th position and moves quickly to 2nd position either by sliding feet to the ball of the foot or as a jump from 5th position to 2nd position)

EN CROIX: In the form of a cross; a four-step movement that begins from a closed position and takes the leg to the front, side, back, and side again

FONDU: To melt (bending and extending of the legs at the same time with one leg supporting the body)

FOUETTÉ: To whip; a quick movement on one leg that requires the dancer to change direction and can be performed in a variety of ways

GLISSADE: To glide; a connecting step that begins and ends in *plié*

GRAND BATTEMENT: A throwing action of the fully extended leg in any direction with controlled lowering

GRAND PLIÉ: A deeper bend (of the knees) bringing the heels of the feet off the floor

PAS DE BOURRÉE: A linking movement done as a series of three quick small steps

PAS DE BOURREÉ PIQUÉ: *Piqué* means "to prick"; a quick step out on one leg to the half-toe or *pointe* position during *pas de boureé*

PAS DE CHAT: Cat's step (because the movement is like a cat's leap); a jump where the legs are lifted and lowered separately, forming a diamond shape in the air

PETIT BATTEMENT: Small beat whereby a pointed foot "beats" in front and back of the calf—just above the ankle—of the opposite leg; this exercise is done with great rapidity

PETIT BATTERIE: A general term to describe a beating of the legs

PIROUETTE: Turn (used to describe a turn, whirl, or spin); "turns" sometimes referred to as *tours*

PLIÉ: To bend (the knee or knees)

POINTE: "Going *en pointe*" is to graduate from soft ballet shoes to the more demanding pointe shoes that have a hard box at the toe in the shape of a cone onto which the tips of the toes balance

RELEVÉ: To rise (used to describe a rise from the whole foot to *demi-pointe* or full *pointe*)

RETIRÉ: Withdrawn (drawing up of the working foot to under the knee)

REVERENCE: A deep curtsey; performed at the end of class, as a mark of thanks and respect

SAUTÉ: To jump off the ground with both feet

SISSONNE: A scissor-like movement where the dancer jumps from two feet to one foot or two feet to two feet

TEMPS LEVÉ: Raised movement; a sharp jump on one foot

TENDU: Stretched; held-out; tight (in which a leg is extended straight out to the front *devant*, back *derrière*, or side *à la seconde*, with the foot fully pointed)